THE CASE OF THE

'CAROUSEL'
KILLER

THE CASE OF THE

'CAROUSEL' KILLER

an Augusta McKee mystery

Susan Moore Jordan

ISBN: 978-1-950625-17-8

Published by Shaggy Dog Productions, LLC

Library of Congress Control Number: 2021910679

Cover design and art by Taylor Van Kooten

Books by Susan Moore Jordan

The *Carousel* Trilogy:
How I Grew Up
Eli's Heart
You Are My Song

Jamie's Children

The Cameron Saga:
Memories of Jake
Man with No Yesterdays

"More Fog, Please"
(non-fiction)

Augusta McKee Mysteries:
The Case of the Slain Soprano
The Case of the Disappearing Director
The Case of the Toxic Tenor
The Case of the Purloined Professor
The Case of the Chrysanthemum Murders
The Case of the Unearthed Evidence
The Case of the 'Carousel' Killer

Table of Contents

'The lightning spark of thought generated
in the solitary mind
awakens its likeness in another mind.'
Thomas Carlyle

for
Ashleigh

with heartfelt thanks for
fanning the flame

Prologue
A Discovery

Pocono Mountains, Pennsylvania
Wednesday, June 8, 1966
11:15 p.m.

Shrill sounds split the air.

A scream, followed by a burst of unintelligible conversation, scrambling footsteps, and then a distant approaching siren.

"What on earth?" Augusta McKee stared at her friend Milly Devereaux. Seated in Augusta's dressing room at the Pocono Playhouse, they stopped in mid-conversation as they gossiped against the usual background noises of departing cars and theatergoers' chatter after a performance of the musical *Carousel*, in which Augusta was playing the role of Nettie Fowler.

All else forgotten, Augusta hastily finished dressing. The two women hurried through the theater to the lobby, where leading actors Evan Llewellyn and Emily Detweiler stood staring toward the parking lot.

As they watched, a Pennsylvania State Police car pulled up, lights swirling. A single Barrett Township police car blocked one exit, a civilian car the other.

Another member of the cast ran by them. "We heard they found a dead body in the parking lot," he yelled out. "Can you believe it?"

Stunned by this information, Augusta, Milly, Evan, and Emily stood together in the theater entrance, watching the chaotic scene unfold as the people in the parking lot grew more agitated and the noise level rose considerably. In a matter of just a few moments, a delightful evening of summer stock theater had turned into a tumultuous crime scene.

"What a horrible end to a lovely evening." Augusta said. "I'd guess at least half the audience has already left. That could be a problem for the police," she mused.

Milly poked her on the shoulder. "We're not in Cincinnati, Augusta. Don't start playing detective. Remember that these cops have no idea who you are."

Some three years earlier, Augusta had met the man who was now her husband, Homicide Detective Malcolm Mitchell of the Cincinnati Police Department. After watching him—and helping him—solve several cases, her observation partly reflected what Malcolm might have thought had he been there.

A member of the Playhouse staff, a portly man in his late sixties, attempted to calm the patrons nearest to him. One of the state troopers turned on the P.A. in his car to address the crowd.

"We need all of you to go back inside, please, while we investigate what happened here tonight," he called out. "Now," he added firmly.

What was left of the audience slowly filed back into the building and took seats, with a number of disgruntled playgoers voicing their objections.

"Oh, great. How can I get in touch with my babysitter?"

"How long is this going to take?"

"I saw the body. It's a woman."

More sirens and lights followed, and moments later two more state police cars arrived on the scene, followed by a civilian vehicle and an ambulance. They all pulled up at the edge of the parking lot and the law enforcement officers quickly exited the cars.

Augusta felt sure one of the men in plain clothes would be the Monroe County Coroner, but she had no idea who the others were.

She turned to the Playhouse staff member. "Who found the woman's body, do you know?"

"Yeah...some guy went to open his car door and almost stepped on her. It was pretty crazy." He ruffled his hair. "Most people didn't stick around, just got the heck out of the parking lot. I guess they figured the cops would show up soon and they didn't want to get stuck here."

Evan touched Augusta's shoulder. "Emily and I might as well change out of our costumes. I would imagine this will take a while." He headed back up the aisle, Emily right behind him.

It was Evan, a colleague and friend from ten years earlier, who had suggested to the director of this production that Augusta might be available to substitute for the actress who would complete the Straw Hat tour of the show.

Miles Richardson, the show's stage manager, stood in the parking lot talking with one of the state troopers who had just arrived. Augusta saw that another of the law enforcement officers had a camera and was preparing to take photographs of the scene. "Forensics team, I would bet," she murmured to Milly.

Miles gestured toward the theater, and he and the trooper strode briskly toward the Playhouse entrance.

Evan and Emily, now in street clothes, rejoined Augusta and Milly in the lobby. "Wonder how long we'll have to wait before we can leave?" Evan asked.

"It's hard to say," Augusta responded. "I'm still having a hard time believing this is happening." Her voice shook slightly. "Not in Barrett Township. Not at the Pocono Playhouse."

Augusta noted the solemn expression on Miles' face as he re-entered with the trooper and they moved to Evan. "Mr. Llewellyn, Trooper LaBar needs to speak with you. He's the lead investigator for this case."

Although dressed in a suit rather than a uniform, broad-shouldered Trooper LaBar projected a military air and spoke with authority. "Mr. Llewellyn, do you know a woman named Joan Cromer?"

"Yes, unfortunately." A pause. Augusta noticed Evan's body tense as he clenched his jaw. He took a deep breath before he continued, "Joan Cromer has been

14

harassing me for over a year; she's apparently obsessed with me. Why do you ask?"

"Because, sir, we found her lying dead next to your car. And there is a note on the windshield addressed to you. Do you have an explanation for that?"

Augusta watched Evan's face drain of color.

"She had followed me here to the Poconos." His voice rose slightly in pitch. "I've told her repeatedly to stay away from me." Evan's eyes darted nervously from LaBar to Augusta.

"When was the last time you saw her, sir?" LaBar busily made notes on a pad as Augusta observed him, thinking how often she'd seen Malcolm do this.

"Last night, after our performance. Before that, Monday night."

"Will you come with me, please? Your identification of the body would be helpful."

Evan glanced at Augusta. "I'd like Mrs. Mitchell to accompany us, if that's possible. She saw Miss Cromer speak to me Monday night. She was aware of what I had been dealing with."

"It will be difficult to see this, Mrs. Mitchell," Trooper LaBar warned her.

"My husband is a homicide detective in Cincinnati, Trooper LaBar. I've seen dead bodies before."

"Very well then, ma'am." The trooper stuffed the pad and pen into his pocket. "A second identification will be useful."

Evan put a hand under Augusta's elbow, holding it tighter than necessary as they moved toward his car.

He's scared, and he should be. He's going to be suspected of this awful crime, thought Augusta. *Interesting that he referred to me as Mrs. Mitchell. The big city detective's wife.*

In the garish light of the parking lot, Joan Cromer's lifeless form lay on gravel and dirt between two cars. Her purse lay a short distance away. Both her shoes had evidently been kicked off as she struggled with her attacker, and she lay on her back, eyes closed, chin tipped upward, arms and legs sprawled, clothing in disarray. Augusta noted that her throat looked red and the skin raw. Her blond, curly hair, so carefully coiffed when Augusta had seen her two nights earlier, was tangled and matted. She shuddered involuntarily as the thought crossed her mind: *This was personal. She was brutalized.* Augusta realized she was touching her own throat involuntarily and forced herself to lower her hand.

She heard Evan's sharp intake of breath and felt his body stiffen as his shoulder touched hers. "My God," he croaked out, obviously shaken. "Yes—that's Joan."

Trooper LaBar eyed both of them. "How long will you be in town, Mr. Llewellyn?"

Miles fielded the question. "Mr. Llewellyn is performing here until the end of next week, Trooper LaBar."

"What time did you arrive at the theater tonight?" LaBar stared intently at Evan.

"Before seven." Evan responded hastily, "And I hadn't left the theater until you asked me to come out here."

LaBar turned to Miles. "We have a lot of work to do, Mr. Richardson, and we need assurance that Mr. Llewellyn won't leave town until we know more."

Evan stepped toward the trooper. "Why would I leave town? I didn't kill Joan," he snapped.

Oh, Evan. Don't get aggressive with a cop. Augusta laid a calming hand on his arm.

"You have my word, Trooper LaBar." Miles added quickly, "And I can confirm I saw Mr. Llewellyn enter the theater before seven tonight. He remained onstage for most of the evening, and I'm sure backstage or in his dressing room at all other times."

"What about the note on my windshield?" Evan asked, "May I see it?"

"Not at the moment. It's evidence," LaBar answered sharply. "As is the car, unfortunately. I need your keys. Is there anything in the car you need?"

"Not...really. It's a rental." Evan fished in his pocket and handed the keys to Trooper LaBar.

"I appreciate your cooperation, Mr. Llewellyn. We'll be in touch." The lead investigator turned and strode toward the ambulance.

"I'm sorry, Miles," Evan said. "I would never in a million years have expected anything remotely like this. It upset me to see Joan here, but who would have ever thought...." his voice trailed off.

"This is not your fault, Evan. I wish you had told me about her, though. Do you need a ride?"

Augusta answered quickly, "Milly and I will take care of that, Miles." She turned to Evan. "I know you're staying at Buck Hill. Let's get your things. I'd like you to come and stay at my Uncle Len's house with us, it's near the Inn. Lenny has tons of room."

Evan stared at Augusta. "I don't want to impose."

"You aren't. You need to be with friends right now." She gazed at him earnestly, then leaned in, lowering her voice. "You do realize you could be a suspect," she said, making sure he understood the gravity of his position.

"I actually could be a...?" The enormity of the situation seemed to register fully as he breathed raggedly, slightly staggering.

Augusta pressed a hand against his back. *Steady, Evan.*

Another sharp intake of breath. "Yes, I guess I must be a suspect." He returned Augusta's gaze. "Thank you...I appreciate the invitation."

She tucked a hand under his elbow and felt his arm trembling as they returned to the theater. "When we get to Uncle Lenny's, Milly will fix some food for us. And you need to get some rest."

And I can keep an eye on you, she thought. *I believe you're about to crack wide open.*

Chapter 1
Anniversary Dinner Aftermath

Cincinnati
May 15, 1966
Some two months earlier

Malcolm Mitchell eased the 1963 sapphire blue Chrysler Imperial into traffic, heading toward Hyde Park. He and his bride of one year, Augusta McKee, had just celebrated their first anniversary at a dinner at Lenhardt's Restaurant in Clifton, hosted by his two sons and their wives and attended by a small group of close friends. Street lights began to flicker on as they drove across four-lane Madison Road, a thoroughfare lined by spacious dwellings and occasional commercial establishments.

Augusta held a box on her lap which contained the remains of the anniversary cake. "What a nice evening. Just about perfect."

"Great of Ryan and Danny to put it together. Certainly more special than the non-event we had planned."

"We did discuss trying to get away for a few days. But you have the Michelson case coming up for trial and we decided making plans wasn't a good idea at the moment, so our agreement to just celebrate later on made sense at the time."

"And that would have been good, too. But I loved us all being together tonight." He gave her a lopsided grin. "Did I tell you how much I like your new dress?"

"I believe you mentioned that," Augusta laughed. A trim five feet nine, she loved clothes and enjoyed the shorter skirts which were popular. This summer dress had cap sleeves and a high waist, and the soft lime green print complemented her hazel eyes and light chestnut hair. White stilettos completed her outfit.

Augusta sighed in contentment, gazing at her husband as she often did, appreciating everything about him: his dedication to his profession as a homicide detective, his keen perception of honor, his intellect, his great sense of humor, and not least, his admiration for what she did as a classical singer and professor of music.

"It's been a wonderful year, you know?" She rested a hand on his arm. "How did I get so lucky to find you?"

"I'm not sure who found who—or whom—but you're right. We're definitely good together." A quick glance from Malcolm in her direction and Augusta melted as always from the intense blue of his gaze. *Oh, and his impressive good looks—tall and lithe, dark hair, and especially those incredible eyes. And that amazing thousand-watt smile that still turns my insides to mush.*

She smiled as the thought of their first, decidedly contentious, meeting crossed her mind, some three years earlier on the campus of Cliffside College, one of two schools in Cincinnati where she taught. A student's body was found in the residence hall, and the girl—a private voice student of Augusta's—had been murdered.

Eventually, Malcolm had enlisted Augusta's assistance as he questioned the residents of Emery Hall; and over time, Augusta had uncovered clues which made it possible for Malcolm to apprehend the killer. A bond of trust and respect grew between them.

It became more than a friendship as they continued to spend time together. Augusta came to appreciate Malcolm's vocation and who he was, a man she had come to love…and he adored her. They'd been together ever since.

The couple pulled into the driveway of their graceful Tudor home in the East Hyde Park section of Cincinnati where their ever-exuberant puppy, Fritz, greeted them joyfully. Malcolm took him out for a walk as Augusta put the cake away and started coffee for them both. She had been a tea drinker before she met Malcolm, but grew to like coffee and enjoyed drinking it with him. One thing she had learned quickly about being with a cop: they drink copious amounts of coffee. *As do Malcolm's sons*, she smiled to herself. *Is coffee loving a gene passed on from generation to generation?*

It meant a great deal to her that her husband's sons from his first marriage had accepted her into their lives completely, telling her they considered her a second mother. Ryan, the older, was an attorney in a prestigious law firm, and his brand-new bride Lacey Stephens, an actress with Parkside Playhouse. Danny, a member of the Cincinnati Police Department, had been married for over a year to Martha Van Camp, a former student of Augusta's. Martha accepted occasional singing engagements but didn't like to leave Danny for long, and Malcolm and Augusta had a sense they wanted to start a family soon. *Which will make me a grandmother*, Augusta mused.

Fritz made a beeline for his mistress once he and Malcolm re-entered the house, and she patted his silky head and flanks and fussed over him. He was an important part of their life and had been for nearly a year now. A Golden Shepherd, Fritz had been to obedience school and done well, but they'd decided it wouldn't hurt for him to have a refresher. He was a big, lovable, slightly goofy animal they both adored, and they reminded each other frequently Fritz was still a puppy, after all…which meant forgiveness for a multitude of puppy missteps.

A grand piano dominated the dining room, and the sliding French doors kept open between the living and dining rooms added to a sense of spaciousness. To the left of the dining room, another set of French doors with glass panes opened into the alcove, Augusta's favorite room.

Mal poured each of them coffee and they took their cups into the living room, Fritz trotting right behind them. Augusta kicked off her stilettos and relaxed into the roomy, comfortable, seafoam green sofa. Malcolm retrieved the shoes so Fritz wouldn't be tempted to misbehave, and placed them out of his reach as the dog curled up at his feet.

Sinking into the sofa beside his bride, Malcolm draped an arm along the back and kissed her softly, moving his lips slowly from her cheek to her neck.

"Oh, that's lovely," she purred, then straightened and turned toward him. "Before we get too distracted, I need to discuss something with you."

He lifted an eyebrow at her. "Nothing serious, I hope. I can't do serious tonight."

"Not serious, no," she chuckled. "More like a request. Or I need to get your opinion on something."

"Okay, I'm all yours."

"I had a phone call earlier today," she began. "I heard from an old friend with whom I once performed at the New York Chautauqua Opera Festival." A sip of coffee. "Evan Llewellyn and I appeared together about ten years ago in an opera by Carlisle Floyd, *Susannah*."

"Evan Llewellyn? A big name in opera these days. I heard him on the radio the other day singing the 'Te Deum' from *Tosca*. Impressive."

"Did you know he's recently been performing in musical theater productions as well? He was sought out by New York producers. A national tour of *South Pacific*, and after that the role of Billy Bigelow in *Carousel* at the new Vivian Beaumont Theater in Lincoln Center."

"Interesting. I hadn't heard that. What'd he call you about?"

"Well…" she shifted her position, tucking her feet up under her and turning to face Malcolm directly. "He's doing Billy Bigelow again on a Straw Hat tour this summer. The way that works is the producer puts a company together in New York to perform in summer theaters in New England and the Northeast for several weeks. This tour is starting at the Pocono Playhouse."

"No kidding. You'd like to go and see it? I know you want to spend some time with your Uncle Lenny up there this summer. Sounds like a perfect opportunity."

"Well…it's a little more than that. It turns out the woman who was engaged for the role of Nettie Fowler for the tour needs time off for her daughter's wedding. A last-minute thing. And since the show opens the first full week of June, they're scrambling to find a replacement." She gazed at Malcolm. "Evan suggested me to the director."

"What will you need to do?"

"I'd have to be there by the second of June. Two rehearsals—one with principals, one with full cast. It would only be for the two-week run at the Playhouse, their original Nettie will be back after that."

She waited for a response, but when none was immediately forthcoming, she continued, "I told him it might not be possible. But I need to let him know tomorrow."

"What about summer school? Do you have any classes?"

"No, only lessons. You know I never have many students during the summer, and one of my grad students can work with the younger singers until I get back. Then

I can double up on lessons if necessary. I know both schools would be agreeable. But I don't know. It's kind of a lot to take on with short notice."

Mal took a gulp of coffee as he considered. "You should do it. I know you'd enjoy it. You haven't been on stage in a couple of years."

"I'm not so sure about leaving you and Fritz for over two weeks, though."

He caressed her face as he again gazed into her eyes. "How about this? The Michelson case is on the docket for late May. So, it should be settled by the second week of June. You know Trevor and Amanda have said over and over they'd love to take care of Fritz for us anytime…this would be a good time for that. I could leave him in their care and come up for the second week of your run."

Trevor Davidson's Golden Shepherd, Caruso, had been Mal and Augusta's house guest in the late summer of 1964 after Trevor had been wounded while on an assignment with Malcolm. Trevor had since married a delightful young woman, a veterinarian's assistant, and the two couples had seen each other socially with dogs in tow. Caruso was Fritz's sire and the dogs obviously enjoyed being together.

"Are you sure? Of course you're right, I would love to do this. You remember I directed *Carousel* at Cliffside last year, so learning the role wouldn't be difficult. Not much dialogue, but two great songs."

"Let's see, Nettie was the leading lady's maiden aunt, correct? Are you sure you want to play an *older* woman?" Malcolm grinned and ruffled her hair. The seven-year age difference between them had been a concern of Augusta's when they first met, though never of Malcolm's. Still, she had felt slightly awkward at first, until she realized his life experience far outweighed hers because of his profession.

"Actually, Nettie is Julie's cousin, but she's older and considered a spinster—a word I dislike. This particular older woman has two of the best-known songs in musical theater, and I see her as strong and independent. She has her own business. Everyone respects and loves her."

"Sounds a lot like a lady I'm acquainted with." Malcolm laughed and kissed her. "Do it, Gus. You'll have a great time, you'll see Uncle Lenny, and I can be there for the second week and stay through that next weekend. We can do some sightseeing…and I made a vow to climb those two cliffs at the Delaware Water Gap, if you recall."

"Oh, that would be so much fun. I'd love to do those hikes with you."

He squinted slightly at her. "Only thing—"

"What?"

"Evan Llewellyn. How well did you know him when you performed in New York?"

"Well…." She hesitated.

"Exactly how well? You were more than friends, I take it."

"We were…close."

"I figured." A slight frown.

Augusta gazed into her cup. *Oh, darn.* A slight sigh. "And I should tell you…I saw him again that year. A couple of times."

Another lifted eyebrow and she added hastily, "But he got married about a year later, and I haven't seen him since. Or even heard from him directly before today."

While Augusta had not been married before, Malcolm was aware she had enjoyed occasional discreet relationships with men over the years. He had even happened to cross paths with the first of these, a French *inspecteur* who had been a musician in Paris when Augusta and her best friend Milly Devereaux spent three years in Europe after graduating from the Cincinnati Conservatory of Music. Mal had never asked her about any others.

"I'm not grilling you about him, Gus. That's in the past." He gave Augusta a lopsided grin. "And we've had this tacit understanding that we don't discuss past relationships either of us had."

"I know that. I admired Evan's talent. He's a nice person. We kind of…well, he's from Carbondale, near Scranton, so we were fellow Pennsylvanians. He had a summer job at Buck Hill Inn in the Poconos when he was in college, so we had that in common. We didn't plan to see each other after our time in Chautauqua. It just…happened."

She sat back and folded her arms. "If this makes you at all uncomfortable, I won't do it. I mean that. Nothing is worth your being upset."

"Augusta McKee, you beat all sometimes," Malcolm pulled her close. "I trust you completely. You have to know that. And you said he's married."

"Well…"

He pulled back and stared at her. "He's divorced?"

They locked eyes for a moment and then burst out laughing.

Augusta snuggled into his arms. "Good heavens, that sounded like a scene from a bad soap opera. Or two teenagers. We're way beyond that."

She giggled. "But I have an idea."

Malcolm nuzzled her neck. "Dare I ask?"

"I'll take Milly with me for that first week. You know how good she is at being the dragon at the gate."

"I trust you." Mal leaned back and grinned. "Not so sure about Llewellyn. I've seen pictures. He looks like a movie star."

"He's also a lot younger than I am."

Mal laughed heartily. "So, that's where the whole 'older woman' thing started, is it?"

"Actually, that could be true. It felt very strange. There were about a half-dozen young women in that company who flirted outrageously with him while they looked daggers at me."

"My beautiful wife who doesn't age. That probably was a little galling for them as well."

"Good genes, a great hair colorist and ballet exercises daily," Augusta laughed. "Plus, now having Fritz drag me all over creation. But thanks for the compliment."

"You know what?" Malcolm tipped Augusta's chin toward him. "Evan Llewellyn sounds like a man of great discernment. He went after the best woman in the company."

Augusta wrapped him in her arms and kissed him thoroughly.

"Don't stop," he murmured.

Chapter 2
The Pocono Playhouse

Pocono Mountains
June 3, 1966

Milly jumped at the opportunity to accompany Augusta to Pennsylvania and spend some time with Leonard Paynter. She had first met Augusta's uncle when the two young women were freshmen at the Conservatory, and Len had made a point of visiting Cincinnati fairly often since then.

Len was only a dozen years older than Augusta, and when he showed up in Cincinnati many of her classmates were quite smitten with the handsome, erudite, and charismatic "older man"— and he obviously enjoyed the attention. Professor of history, world traveler, and environmental activist, Lenny's charm kept them entertained while he himself didn't play favorites— except for Augusta's closest friend Milly. An accomplished pianist, Millicent Devereaux eventually established herself as not only an in-demand concert artist but also as one of the finest teachers in the U.S. Lenny looked on her as another niece—sometimes referring to her fondly as "Madcap Milly."

During the Spanish flu epidemic of 1918, Lenny was dispatched by Augusta's grandparents to move Augusta and her mother from Philadelphia, one of the cities most stricken by the disease, to their home in the relative safety of the Pocono Mountains. Augusta's mother, who later died from the flu, refused to leave her husband but sent Augusta.

Eight-year-old Augusta spent nearly a year in the Poconos with the uncle she saw sometimes as an extension of her mother, sometimes as an older brother. He taught her to swim, canoe, ride a horse, shoot skeet, climb trees and mountains. And play bridge, backgammon, and chess. After her father took her back to Philadelphia, Augusta spent every summer with Lenny and her grandparents until she left for Cincinnati and music school. Len and Augusta managed to get together at least once a year. He missed Augusta's wedding because of an extended trip to the Far East, but Augusta and Mal had visited him in Pennsylvania for a weekend only a few months earlier.

"We can drive up to Carbondale while Augusta's rehearsing if you'd like to see it." In the spacious kitchen in his Buck Hill home Len briskly dried dishes as Milly washed.

"I can't even imagine how those people live," she replied. "How long did you say this coal mine fire has been burning?"

"It started sometime in the early 1940s, so it's been going for at least twenty years."

Augusta overheard their conversation as she came downstairs, preparing to head for her rehearsal at the Pocono Playhouse. From the time Len met them at the Avoca airport near Scranton, he had captivated them with stories about the Carbondale underground mine fire and what the environmental group he belonged to was trying to accomplish. When she had called Lenny, Augusta said they could rent a car, but he told her he'd have a car available to them and besides, he'd like to pick them up.

Milly and Len continued making plans as Augusta stood in the kitchen doorway. "I'm not sure when I'll be back," she remarked. "I think the cast is being treated to dinner."

"How can people live with a fire burning under their feet like that?" Milly handed Len the next plate.

"It is definitely hard to imagine," Len swiped the plate vigorously. "You know, I've asked myself that more than—"

"Hello, you two!" Augusta pronounced loudly, and they finally stopped and glanced her way. "Sorry to interrupt your fun, but I wanted to let you know not to expect me for dinner. There's a buffet for the cast after we finish rehearsing."

"Sorry, honey." Len gave her a hug. "That's fine. Maybe Milly and I can go out. You have a key to the cottage, right?"

Augusta dangled the set of keys he had provided, car and house, to show him she did.

"As I was saying before we were so rudely interrupted, it's been very tough for them," Len resumed his conversation with Milly. "They never know when their house might be the next one to be demolished."

As Augusta backed out of Len's driveway, she mused about the homes in Buck Hill being referred to as "cottages." Len's large home had a rustic exterior, decorative logs giving it something of the appearance of a cabin, but it contained ten rooms, including six bedrooms, and three full baths. *Hardly a cottage,* she smiled to herself.

Driving to the Playhouse through the picturesque, wooded roads of Barrett Township awakened warm feelings of nostalgia in Augusta. She rolled down her window to let the fresh, clean mountain air completely envelop her, the invigorating air she so well remembered. She slowed the car and opened her senses to sounds and fragrances so unlike those of a busy city. *Listen to that! No traffic sounds. Everyone should visit the Poconos and experience this,* she thought.

While the Playhouse hadn't opened until the 1940s, Augusta had visited Lenny even after she'd started teaching in Cincinnati, enjoying the excellent productions featuring well-known performers. She had to admit she felt a thrill to think she'd be on that stage herself for the next two weeks. While Augusta had directed the annual musical theater production for several years at Cliffside College, it had been a long time since she had performed in one, not since her graduate school days at Indiana University. And that barely qualified as a musical since it was a Gilbert and Sullivan operetta, *The Mikado*. It was a nice change for Augusta, to step away for a short time from her responsibilities and just be a member of the cast, something she hadn't done for many years.

She slowed down to turn onto a side road to reach the Playhouse, seeing the tall fly tower first through the trees, then the rustic, barn-like building with the wide porch and its proud letters POCONO PLAYHOUSE across the front of the porch roof.

Augusta's face lit up as she spotted Evan Llewellyn watching for her. *He's hardly changed at all.* It struck her how much he resembled Malcolm physically: both were lithely muscular and over six feet tall. There the resemblance ended. Mal had dark, almost black, hair and blue eyes, and Augusta thought of him as "ruggedly handsome." Evan boasted more classic features, startlingly gray eyes, and lighter brown hair. *Malcolm was right to describe Evan as "movie star handsome,"* she thought. Evan waved as she pulled into the parking lot and strode to open her car door with a grand flourish and a broad smile.

"Professor McKee. How nice to see you again. And as always, dressed as smartly as a fashion model. Be careful with those beautiful stilettos—the parking lot isn't paved."

No, he hasn't changed.

He extended a hand to assist her from the car.

"Mr. Llewellyn. I feel as though I should ask for your autograph. I remember predicting ten years ago you'd have a major career in opera. And it isn't a surprise you've become a matinee idol."

Evan laughed, holding her elbow as they headed into the Playhouse. "Well, I guess you're talking about my new venture into musical theater. I hope everyone in the audiences appreciates my performance."

"I'm sure they do, but you have always especially appealed to the ladies."

She glanced around as they crossed the deep porch and passed through the vestibule into the auditorium. Inside, the rustic barn revealed a comfortable and well-appointed theater with about 300 plush red seats. A piano on the floor in front of the stage would be joined by several other instruments to create an ensemble to accompany the performances. Augusta saw the set designer putting finishing touches on the compact but beautifully decorated carousel which the show demands for the first scene. Evan introduced her to Jim Lawrence, who beamed at her reaction as he showed her how it revolved.

"This is absolutely remarkable. You're a genius," she commented, impressed with his design and the careful detail on the expertly hand-painted horses.

She next met the show's directors, including the man she'd be working most closely with, stage manager Miles Richardson—tall, gangly, seemingly in constant motion and unfailingly enthusiastic. Augusta liked him immediately.

The stage director would return to New York after opening night, leaving Miles as stage manager to oversee the remainder of the run. Augusta first worked with the director and music director, getting the blocking for her scenes and staging for her songs, as they also agreed on tempos and musical nuances. Evan helped Miles read lines of other characters during Augusta's blocking rehearsal.

During a break for lunch the wardrobe mistress commandeered Augusta for her costume fittings. "Oh, we have lots of items that will work for you," Laurie Benefield said as she wrote down Augusta's measurements. "What are you, about five feet nine or ten? Most of these dresses have deep hems. I learned to do that early on."

She led Augusta to one section of the large wardrobe department and pulled out several items. "I know you only need two, but for fun, why don't we give Nettie a costume change before the end of Act One?"

Laurie hung them on a rack so Augusta could examine them. Similar in style, ankle length, full skirts, three-quarter length sleeves, each in a different print fabric. A long white apron which could go over any of them.

"I'd love it," Augusta laughed. She admired the artistry with which the costumes had been constructed. "These are beautiful. Did you build them?"

"These two. The other has been here for a while." Laurie put her hands on her hips and gazed at Augusta.

"What?"

"I love your hair. Beautiful shade of chestnut and you have a great stylist, but it's hardly 1840s' New England whaling village." Both women laughed.

"No, I guess not. Too short to pull back and add a bun, I think." Augusta ran her fingers through her hair. "What about a wig?"

"I have one that will work," Laurie said. She went to a cabinet marked WIGS, opened it, and quickly located the one she had in mind. Medium brown, and styled from the period: deep waves, a center part, and curls down the back of the head.

Augusta bent over, fixed the wig to her head, and stood up, gazing at herself in the floor length mirror. "Instant Nettie. It's perfect."

Lunch was waiting for them in the theater, and other cast members were beginning to arrive to do a run of the entire show without the chorus or tech crew on hand. Augusta noticed the young soprano playing the role of Julie Jordan—the cousin of her character, Nettie Fowler—frequently gazing raptly at Evan. He was attentive to her, but seemed to be trying to keep it light.

Another break, and the company headed to a nearby family resort for a buffet dinner. Evan again waited for Augusta when she pulled into the parking lot. "We haven't had a chance to catch up," he commented. "Let's do that during dinner."

"If you're sure. I feel I'll be stealing you from sweet Emily Detweiler," she teased.

He grinned wryly. "Probably a good thing. I believe she'd like an offstage romance, but it's not happening."

"Emily's doing an excellent job with her role. And she's lovely."

"And she's also a year out of grad school and just twenty-four. She could be my daughter."

Augusta lifted an eyebrow at him and he laughed.

"I know exactly what prompted that remark," she said. "We do have a lot to talk about, don't we?"

The sumptuous buffet was set up on a deck, and seating was casual at tables or even near the deck railing, which was broad enough to comfortably hold a table setting. Evan and Augusta went through the line filling their plates.

Augusta was hungry and helped herself to potato salad, cheeses and vegetables from the antipasto platter, fruit, a small slice of both ham and cheese, and a dinner roll. Evan stuck with a serving of tossed salad, fruit, and hearty slices of beef and ham.

The dessert table, laden with a wide variety of cakes and pies, looked tempting, but Augusta decided against indulging, as did Evan.

"I see you still avoid bread and desserts," Augusta commented.

He grinned. "More than ever." They each picked up a glass of iced tea, and Evan motioned toward the railing. "Let's go over there, shall we?"

They seated themselves at a distance from the other cast members, who were engrossed in lively conversations punctuated by occasional outbursts of laughter. Emily glanced at Evan for a moment, then turned her attention to the young tenor playing the role of Enoch Snow.

Evan and Augusta ate in companionable silence for a few minutes as dusk approached, turning the sky slowly to soft shades of darker blue. The sounds wafting through the air changed as bird songs grew quieter and the breeze through the trees became more audible.

"It's beautiful here. Didn't you tell me you grew up in this area?" Evan sipped his drink.

"I spent summers here from the time I was a child until I graduated from high school. So, yes, in a way, I did. My family owned a summer cottage which is now my Uncle Len's home. I'm staying with him for these two weeks."

He turned to gaze at her. "Ten years. It hardly seems that long."

"Carlisle Floyd's *Susannah*. You were extraordinary in the role of Olin Blitch. What fun to play a truly bad guy. Another baritone operatic villain, but with a twist."

"It was a bit of a stretch for me. I've seen Norman Treigle in the role. He's perfect."

"You were excellent."

"I was distracted." He grinned. "I had met this soprano I was definitely smitten with, but she wouldn't give me the time of day."

"Not true. We had a lovely few weeks together." *Oh, dear. Where is he going with this?*

He leaned in closer. "Do you remember the day we first met?"

She gave him a sidelong glance. "Indeed I do."

"I'd seen you perform in *Carmen* the night before. For me, Frasquita was the best thing about that production."

She laughed. "So you said."

"We had lunch together. Then dinner." He rested a hand on the arm of her chair.

"Yes, I recall."

Evan smiled, his eyes twinkling. "We did a lot together."

Augusta laughed again. "That surprised me." She glanced around to be sure no one was in earshot. "I mean, that you wanted to be with me. After all, I was at least ten years older than you, and there were several lovely young ladies who were falling all over themselves vying for your attention."

"That age thing never bothered me," Evan shrugged. "But I understand better why you reacted as you did when I have a much younger woman making googly eyes at me."

"You mean Emily."

"Exactly. But it's a lot more than ten years." He gazed into the distance. "I was married for a while."

"Yes, I heard."

"It might have been a rebound thing...from you. About a year after the last time you and I were together. My ex reminded me of you in some ways. A young, aspiring singer. Some physical resemblance—tall and slim with hazel eyes. But nothing like you in other ways." He hesitated. "The important ways. Too self-centered. No sense of humor. The marriage lasted two years."

"That must have been a difficult time for you."

He tipped his head, speaking softly. "What's difficult, Augusta, is that I find I still have feelings for you." When she didn't respond, he continued, "And the man you married—he's about my age. What was different?"

And here we are. I think this is what Malcolm suspected could happen. Think fast, Augusta.

41

"*I* was different." She gazed at him earnestly. "Maybe partly because he's not a musician. Mal loves music. He even loves opera. But you know what he does."

"You told me when I called. He's a cop."

"He's a homicide detective who appreciates what I do. I admire him immensely for what he does. We both care about what happens in our city and to the people who live there."

"You move in different worlds."

"That's true. But I've—this may sound strange—I've actually helped him solve some cases."

"That doesn't surprise me. You're a brilliant woman. Beautiful, talented, and smart as hell."

She chuckled. "Same old Evan. But you're laying it on a bit thick, even for you."

"No, I'm not. It's all true," he insisted. "How did I let you get away, anyhow?"

Augusta remained quiet for a moment. "We enjoyed each other for a time. I believe that's what was meant to be."

Evan gazed skyward with a pensive expression on his face as Augusta waited for his response.

"What changed when you met your detective? How were you different?"

Augusta saw he was looking for a serious answer. She thought for a long moment before replying.

"We met on the campus of one of the colleges where I teach. He was working on the murder of a young woman who was a student of mine. You know—our first meeting was quite confrontational. Malcolm challenged me in a way I've seldom been challenged. I thought him arrogant and rude at our first encounter. As it happened, I was able to provide him with information which made it possible for him to arrest the killer."

"And now you're married to him."

"I am. As I grew to know him, I realized how much I was drawn to him. His intuition, his wit, his strength, his surprising tenderness. I asked him once why he'd become a homicide detective. I'll never forget his response, that he believed his vocation was one of the most cognitively satisfying on God's earth. Solving a murder was like putting a puzzle together, and when the last piece was in place, he had made a real difference. I came to appreciate that."

"You mentioned you helped him solve that case. And some others since?"

She smiled wryly. "Not always with his approval, especially at first. But knowing him opened new doors for me—and I walked right through them." Augusta paused and added softly, "And I soon realized I was falling in love with him. I knew I had met the man I would spend the rest of my life with."

Evan's eyes narrowed. "Does he know about us— about our history?"

"Yes, of course. I told him." She laid a hand on his arm. "I also told him you're a good person. And a fine performer. He'll be here for the second week of our run."

A rueful smile, and after a short silence Evan gave his lips a final wipe with his napkin and stood. "Well, as they say, timing is everything. Once I thought of you for Nettie and heard your voice on the phone, I remembered the special time we were together. And I realized that for me at least, our relationship had never been fully resolved. I knew you were married and that it was a long shot…but I needed to find out once and for all."

Augusta gazed directly at him. "I'm sorry, Evan." She hesitated. "Still friends?"

"Of course. Always."

Chapter 3
Offstage Drama

Sunday, June 5

Augusta donned her dancing shoes late Sunday morning to meet with Miles and the women of the ensemble to learn her choreography for "June Is Bustin' Out All Over." The fact that lanky, loose-limbed Miles was teaching the choreography surprised her, but he proved to be a fine dancer and a good teacher.

"Be kind," she said to him as she nervously stood center stage. "You don't want to know how many years it's been since I danced on a stage."

"You still dance, though?" Straight-legged, he bent from the waist and placed his hands flat on the floor.

"In a way. I do my barre exercises daily." She smiled to herself. *I also sometimes give private dance performances for Malcolm, something not for public knowledge.*

Miles put them through their paces, and it pleased Augusta that she picked up the routine quickly. The other women were encouraging and seemed delighted to have her as part of their show family. During the catered lunch break she took advantage of the chance to get to know some of her fellow cast members. It reminded her what an ensemble effort a good show needed to be.

The men joined them after lunch for the dress rehearsal, which went smoothly until intermission, when Evan's knife was missing for a time. It had been misplaced quite by accident, but he was obviously annoyed. Augusta noticed many people in the cast seemed uncomfortable around him. *Is he playing diva here? The famous opera singer setting himself apart from the crowd?*

***

Just before the curtain rose Monday night for the opening of the show, Augusta had a moment of elation combined with a brief chill of fear as she heard the audience quiet when the house lights dimmed. She had always felt this before a performance, and she knew it meant all her senses were on high alert. The curtain lifted, she took a deep breath—and it was Nettie Fowler who stepped onto the stage.

Augusta relished being onstage again, and being a member of the cast and not in charge was a delight. Leading the rollicking ensemble number "June is Bustin' Out All Over" was great fun and went perfectly; that intense choreography session had paid off. In the second act, the reception she received after her big solo, "You'll Never Walk Alone," was immensely gratifying.

Carousel's opening night was heartily applauded by a sold-out house, and a wine and cheese party was set up afterward on the porch of the Playhouse for cast and guests from the audience. Milly and Len attended the performance but didn't stay for the party. They had a breakfast meeting the next day with Len's environmental group, the Wyoming Valley Land Reclamation Organization, and had to drive to Scranton fairly early. A beaming Len told Augusta how much he had enjoyed seeing her onstage again. He hadn't attended a performance of hers since the first time she appeared at the Brevard Music Festival some fifteen years earlier. Milly proclaimed it one of the best productions of *Carousel* she'd ever seen, and Augusta "without a doubt the best Nettie ever!"

Augusta enjoyed mingling with the mostly local crowd, some of whom she remembered meeting all those years ago during her high school days. One elderly couple excitedly hurried up to her. "Maggie and Jake Downes, Augusta. Do you remember us? We live three houses down from your Uncle Lenny."

"Of course I do. How wonderful to see you again." As they talked, Augusta became aware of an attractive blond woman nearby, staring unwaveringly at Evan. As she watched, Evan moved to her and they exchanged words. The woman rested a hand on Evan's chest as she gazed up at him. Augusta saw Evan frown and yank her hand off his chest. The blond woman moved even closer, chattering at him, attempting to touch his face, and he glanced around uncomfortably.

Who is she? Augusta turned her attention again to the Downeses, but soon became aware that Evan had taken the woman's elbow and quickly escorted her off the porch and away from the party.

Now what's that all about? Evan seems quite disturbed. The Downeses turned to speak to friends, giving Augusta the opportunity to slip away and step off the porch, searching to see where Evan and the woman were. She stayed in the shadows, moving closer to listen to their conversation.

"I've told you repeatedly, Joan, I don't want to see you again," Evan took a step away from the woman, fighting to keep his voice level. "You have to leave. You have to stop this."

"I can't stop loving you, Evan," the distraught-sounding woman replied, staring at him. "We have a future together, you know that. We belong together. We have to make plans."

Still in shadow, Augusta moved slightly closer in order to see Joan's face.

Arms folded across his chest, Evan glared at the woman, his jaw set firmly. "We don't have a future together. We don't even have a past. You're not in love with me."

Joan gazed at him with unwavering adoration. "How could I not be in love with you? After all those amazing times we spent together." She extended both arms toward him.

"One weekend, Joan. And that was a mistake." Evan caught her hands and pressed them down to her sides. "I made it very clear nothing would come of it." Augusta was surprised to hear his voice shake. "Yet you've been following me ever since. Please leave." Evan made a strong gesture with his hand, as if pushing her away.

Joan reached out and caught his arm. "You know you don't mean that, Evan. You and I are meant to be together. Forever." Her voice rose slightly, starting to become shrill.

Evan attempted to remove Joan's hand from his arm as he took a step back, his voice rising in turn. "I never want to see you again. Do you want me to take some kind of legal action?"

"Why would you do that? I'd never harm you. I adore you. I only want us to be together." She stumbled forward as she desperately clung to his arm, now with both hands.

Evan firmly pulled her hands away. "Get out of here, Joan." Jaw still clenched, he spoke roughly. "I don't know what kind of obsession you have, but stay away from me. I mean it!" He turned abruptly to walk away from her.

As Joan started to follow Evan, Augusta realized Joan had seen her standing nearby. She hesitated, glaring at Augusta murderously before she turned and headed for the parking lot.

Startled, Augusta caught a breath. *My word. What a one-eighty, from whining at Evan to shooting daggers in my direction. She seems unhinged.*

Evan had seen Augusta as well and moved to her. The expression of confusion and alarm on his face prompted her to place a sympathetic hand on his arm. *Good Lord. He's shaking. This woman IS obsessed with him. She's been—harassing him. Could she be…stalking him?*

They heard Joan's car start and Evan pulled a handkerchief from his pocket. "I'm sorry you witnessed that." He blotted perspiration from his face and forehead. "I don't know what to do about her." The words spilled out in a rush. "It started nearly a year ago, nothing more than a casual weekend. I made it clear that was all it would be."

Evan took a few steps further away from the porch. "I was touring with *South Pacific* at the time, and she showed up two or three times over the next few months, expecting to renew the relationship."

"I can see how upsetting this is to you." Augusta clenched her hands together, a clutch of anxiety spilling into the pit of her stomach.

He stopped pacing and faced her. "I was very firm and told her to please stay away from me. Then a couple of months later while I was at Lincoln Center doing *Carousel*, she showed up for the first week. *Every damn night.*" On each of the final three words he smacked his right fist into his open left palm.

"I don't know how to handle this," he groaned, hands in the air.

"Have you talked to a lawyer? You know this is harassment, right? You might have some legal recourse."

Evan stared hard at Augusta. "She hasn't actually threatened me. What's the term? Threatened me with bodily harm." He sighed heavily and ran a hand over the back of his neck. "And even if she had, I'm not sure cops would take me seriously. Men are expected to handle this kind of crazy female behavior on their own."

"Who is she, anyway? I heard you call her 'Joan.'"

"Her name is Joan Cromer." Evan's mouth twisted as he attempted a grim smile. "She happens to be from your city—Cincinnati."

"What else has she said to you?"

Another sigh. "She claims I asked her to marry me. Not true. I made it clear from the start that what happened between us was casual—nothing more."

Augusta rested a hand on his shoulder. "Honestly, Evan, you need to talk to an attorney. I believe she *is* threatening you. Maybe not physically, but she's already done some emotional damage to your peace of mind. I know an excellent attorney in Cincinnati we could speak with, Milly's beau Garrett Stoddard. I think he could give you some advice."

He nodded. After a moment Augusta added, "You should go back into the party."

Evan stared at her, a strange, almost forlorn expression crossing his face. "I don't feel much like rejoining the festivities."

"I don't blame you, but if you don't there'll be talk." Augusta paused. "Don't stay long. I'll stick close by you and we'll leave in about fifteen minutes."

A wry grin. "Now *that* for sure will create some talk."

"So what?" Augusta tossed her head. "Everybody in the cast knows we're friends. Some may have guessed we were more at one time. Who cares? Let them talk."

Evan relaxed slightly and offered her his arm. "Augusta McKee to the rescue."

"Happy to oblige." She took his arm, squeezing it lightly. "I'll give Garrett a call tomorrow and let you know what he says."

They took another moment to regain their composure before returning to the party.

And after I phone Garrett, I may call Malcolm and see what he can find out about the definitely disturbed Joan Cromer. It can't hurt.

***

Tuesday night provided another smooth run as well as another enthusiastic audience. Some cast members agreed to meet at a local restaurant for a late supper. Augusta and Emily arrived at the same time.

"Have I told you I see you as the perfect Julie Jordan?"

Emily flushed with pleasure at the compliment. "Thank you…but perfect? I doubt that."

"Well, at least nearly perfect—will you accept that? I can't think of a thing I'd suggest you doing differently. You seem to see this show exactly as I do: it's really more about Julie than Billy."

Emily laughed. "We're both renegades, then. I do think Julie needs to be the focus more than Billy." She indicated seats for them. "Let's save one for Evan, shall we?"

Augusta nodded in agreement. "I directed this show not long ago, and that's exactly how I approached it."

"Julie's strong love has to be evident for the audience to better deal with the element of domestic abuse," Emily continued. "Julie's love for Billy is unwavering and all-encompassing. I believe she's convinced that will eventually lead him to being able to love her as strongly in return."

Just as you, Emily, are hoping your love for Evan will break down the barrier he's put up between you, Augusta thought. It hadn't surprised Augusta that Evan had added yet another adoring female to a long list. *Oh, you are a charmer,* she thought.

As if on cue, Evan joined them, appearing slightly annoyed when he took the seat between the two women.

"Joan Cromer?" Augusta asked in a low voice.

Evan nodded. "She tried to speak to me when I went to my car. I completely ignored her."

"Good choice. Maybe she'll get the message and get out of town."

"From your lips to God's ears." He turned to speak with Emily.

The entire first week of the run was sold out, largely due to the popularity of the leading man. On Wednesday night, the effusive audience greeted the cast of *Carousel* with a standing ovation as the curtain rose for their final bow. Augusta remained backstage for a few moments as she complimented Evan on his portrayal of Billy Bigelow.

"I know I've said it before, but your Billy has such depth. Not easy to achieve with a musical theater character, but I think we see the hurt he's experienced in his short life."

53

Evan grinned as he blotted his face and the back of his neck with his handkerchief. He embraced Augusta briefly. "Coming from you, that's quite a compliment." Their eyes met; a shared memory of their first meeting, when Evan had admired Augusta's performance skills and eventually enlisted her assistance with his role of Olin Blitch in the opera *Susannah*.

"We discussed having dinner together tonight with your friend Milly and your Uncle Len. Are we still on?"

"Yes, I made reservations."

"Oh, good. I'm looking forward to spending time with them."

Evan turned to Emily. "I guess we should head for the lobby."

At the Pocono Playhouse, leading performers sometimes greeted audience members in the lobby and made themselves available for autographs and photos following a performance. A group from the Lehigh Valley had requested a "meet-and-greet" with Evan and Emily.

"Yes, let's," Emily responded, gazing at Evan with something more than admiration. Augusta watched them move away and retreated to her dressing room.

"As I said on Monday, you've still got it, my dear." Milly, who once again had been in the audience, stuck her head in the door. "Terrific performance."

Augusta smeared cold cream on her face. "I think an older maiden relative is a perfect role for me at this point in my career." She yanked several tissues from a box and vigorously wiped her face as they both laughed.

"You had the audience in tears with 'You'll Never Walk Alone,'" Milly remarked. "Beautifully done."

Augusta waved a hand. "It's that scene. It's such excellent writing from Rodgers and Hammerstein, and the audience needs to cry at that point. It's a treat to sing it."

"Still…you made it special."

"Thanks, Milly." Augusta deftly applied street makeup as she continued, "Isn't Evan something? Quite an accomplishment to do musical theater as well as he does opera." She shrugged out of her costume.

"Well, he's certainly easy on the eyes. One of the best-looking men I've ever seen."

"Why, Millicent. I'm surprised at you, being more aware of him as a hunk than a great baritone."

"Well, I may be an *older* woman, but I'm not dead," Milly chuckled. "Was he that gorgeous when you performed with him ten years ago?"

"To be honest, he hasn't changed much at all." Augusta slipped her dress over her head and stepped into her stilettos. "What's the plan for dinner? The Top Hat, right?"

"Yes. I'm supposed to call Len once we get there," Milly said.

Then they heard the sirens.

Chapter 4
Strategies

Thursday, June 9
2:00 a.m.

"I was getting worried," Len met them at the door, his eyes widening when he saw Evan with two suitcases.

"Evan needs to stay with us," Augusta told him. "I'll explain later. Can you please show him to a room?"

"Of course." Len reached for one of the suitcases. "Follow me."

Milly headed for the telephone.

"It's two o'clock in the morning," Augusta reminded her. "Don't you think you should wait until the sun comes up before you call Garrett?"

"This is an honest-to-God emergency, Augusta. He won't mind. He can get on the phone and start making travel arrangements. He needs to get here as soon as possible."

Too keyed up to even consider sleep, Augusta went into the kitchen and started a pot of coffee. She couldn't wipe the sight of Joan Cromer's dead body out of her mind; every time she closed her eyes, it reappeared.

I have to wonder if anyone else at that after party saw the argument between Evan and Joan. And he said she showed up again Tuesday night. We need to know about that confrontation. And if anyone else witnessed what I did Monday night, they very well might have thought he was angry enough to strangle her.

"Okay, I'll tell her. Thanks, counselor. You're the best.... I love you, too." Milly joined Augusta in the kitchen. "Okay, he's going to try to get a flight up here tomorrow. Well, later today. He says absolutely he wants to help, and he's licensed to practice in Pennsylvania, so that won't be a problem."

"What else? You said something like 'I'll tell her'…what was that about?"

Milly ran a hand over her salt-and-pepper curls and gave Augusta a lopsided grin. "Well, thanks to your call yesterday he knew the victim was the same woman who's obsessed with Evan and has been harassing him. Garrett says this probably only happened because you're in town."

Both women chuckled.

"Not true," Augusta sighed. "Poor Evan. Do you know anything about women who do this? I've seldom seen someone so determined…so fixated on something."

Milly set out cups for four and glanced questioningly at Augusta.

"Do you think Evan will want to talk some more tonight? He may be ready to collapse."

Len joined them and confirmed exactly that. "Evan asked me to tell you he's exhausted and just wants to try to get some sleep. He did tell me what happened, though."

Augusta poured coffee for the three of them.

"I called Garrett," Milly told Len. "He'll be here as soon as he can get a flight out, either to Avoca or Allentown. Or even to Newark."

Len nodded. He had met Garrett during Christmas when he visited Augusta and Malcolm, and it became an instant friendship. "I'll pick him up and fill him in. What else do I need to tell him?"

Augusta sipped her coffee, two sugars and a lot of cream. She still couldn't handle black coffee. "I've been thinking about a couple of things that may be important."

Len and Milly waited for her to continue. "First of all, I'll be surprised if the autopsy doesn't show Joan was strangled. I saw her body. I can't unsee it. The way her head was angled, the raw skin on her throat." She shuddered. "I think her killer was enraged. I'm surprised he didn't break her neck."

"Maybe he did," Len responded grimly. "We'll probably find out this afternoon."

"Something else that concerns me. She was killed right next to Evan's car. She must have parked after she arrived at the Playhouse and found the car, planning to wait there after the show to talk to him. That may be what happened Tuesday night as well. He told me she tried to speak with him and he ignored her. It would be helpful to know more about that confrontation." Augusta took another swallow of coffee.

"And there's this: they're surely going to investigate exactly where Evan was during the whole evening. You may remember there's a fairly long stretch of time in the first act when Evan's character, Billy, is not onstage. Almost everyone else is. Probably a good twenty minutes."

"Didn't you tell me Miles covered that with the state trooper?"

"He did, but I doubt if he really knows exactly where Evan was during that time. Theoretically, he could have left the theater, seen Joan, killed her, and come back inside."

"Good God, Augusta." Len stared at her.

"Oh, I'm sure he didn't do it. But he *could* have, timewise. Another thing—there was no blood on her body. I don't know if the coroner will find anything under her fingernails if she resisted her attacker. But again—no blood on her hands."

"You thought to look for that when you saw her?" Len was dumbfounded.

"Well, I am married to a homicide detective who shares stuff with me. I'd been with Evan numerous times during the performance, and he was acting normally and didn't have any scratches on his face or hands that I recall seeing."

Milly poured herself another half cup of coffee. "If he'd gone outside and strangled her, he would have had to go onstage and sing an aria only a few minutes later. I don't know how he could possibly have done that. And he sounded great."

Len asked, "An aria? *Carousel* is a musical, not an opera."

"I think Milly's correct. Billy Bigelow's 'Soliloquy' is an aria. Long, somewhat complicated, and at the end, vocally demanding. Not something a baritone can just croon his way through." Augusta took their cups into Len's kitchen to rinse them out.

"We all need to get some sleep. Tomorrow may be a very long day." Milly stood and stretched.

She waited for Augusta to re-emerge from the kitchen before going upstairs. "This has to feel at least a little awkward. Here you are in the same house with an old lover—who happens to be one foxy dude—and he's in the room next door to yours. And I see how he looks at you. I think maybe you should bunk in with me tonight."

Augusta smiled wryly. "Thanks, but it's not necessary. The operative word there is 'old.' Evan is a friend who may be in big trouble and needs help. He and I are quite clear that we are just friends. Good heavens, Milly, you know how much I adore Malcolm. Speaking of whom…I plan to call him first thing in the morning to tell him exactly what happened tonight. And to see what he can learn about Joan Cromer. The woman was definitely disturbed."

***

"I have some bad news. A woman who has avidly been pursuing Evan all over the eastern United States was in town to see him in *Carousel*. Last night her body was

61

discovered in the parking lot at Pocono Playhouse." Augusta was still in her night clothes, curled up on the sofa in Lenny's living room.

"She was strangled, and her name was Joan Cromer," Malcolm replied.

Augusta gasped in surprise. "How on earth did you know that?"

"I got a phone call about two o'clock this morning from the CPD homicide detective on call last night. It seems the Pennsylvania State Trooper who is investigating the case met a lady at the Playhouse who is married to a homicide detective in Cincinnati named Mitchell. He mentioned that when he called for a notifier to go to the Cromer home."

"Oh."

"Why didn't you call me?"

"Because it was two o'clock in the morning. How would I know you'd become involved in this?"

"Yeah. Ron called and told me, 'You ain't gonna believe this, but....' He was right. It was tough to believe. I offered to go with him so his partner didn't have to get up."

"So why didn't you call me?"

"Because it was after three o'clock in the morning." They both chuckled.

"Well, anyway, I'm calling you now to give you some details." Augusta proceeded to explain about the altercation she had witnessed on Monday night, and continued with Evan's account of Joan's obsession and subsequent pursuit.

She shifted on the sofa so she could read the notes she had made. "Evan says she showed up in Indianapolis when he was performing as Emile de Becque in *South Pacific* on a national tour. She's a very attractive woman, Mal. They ended up spending the weekend together, and she told him she lives in Cincinnati where she works as an event planner."

"Does she have her own business?"

"That I don't know. I have time today. I could make some calls and see if I can find out for you."

"You've done that kind of thing before," Mal chuckled. "I'm sure you can come up with some story as to why you're trying to reach her."

"I'll let you know if I have any luck." She looked again at her notes. "Evan says she never told him her age, but he thinks she's about thirty-five. She told him she graduated from Withrow High School in 1950. Sixteen years ago. She never mentioned college. She may have gone to some kind of trade school, or maybe even the University of Cincinnati. If she was good at what she did, secretarial skills might be helpful. But really, social skills would probably be the most important for that job."

Malcolm was quiet for a moment and Augusta could visualize him making notes on his pad. The mental image made her catch a breath and feel an ache in her chest. *Oh, I miss him so much.* Aloud she said, "When do you think you might be able to get here?"

"Not before sometime this weekend at the earliest, but honestly, that's unlikely. I'm scheduled to testify tomorrow afternoon. Trevor and Amanda are planning to pick Fritz up Monday morning, and I have a flight reservation for Monday afternoon."

"Please come as soon as you can. I don't think this looks good at all for Evan. He's scared, Mal." She wound the phone cord around her hand and added softly, "And I miss you."

A pause, and he cleared his throat before he replied. "I miss you, too. I promise I'll get there as soon as possible. In the meantime, you'll have Garrett there tonight."

"Yes, I'm grateful for that. I'm really afraid someone may have seen Joan and Evan having an argument at some point." Augusta shifted her position again, resting her arm across the back of the sofa and stretching out her legs. "Maybe not what I witnessed Monday night, but he said she showed up again on Tuesday. He said he didn't even speak to her, just got in his car and drove away."

She looked again at the notes she'd made. "Here are some thoughts I jotted down: Who knows what Joan might have told other people about her fantasy relationship with Evan? And the lead investigator for the Pennsylvania State Police has obviously contacted the local news outlets—Joan's death was the headline this morning in the *Pocono Record*. With a box on the front page asking members of the audience Wednesday night who had seen or heard anything to contact the State Police. The investigative unit is located in the Mt. Pocono barracks."

"That makes sense. You told me you thought at least half the audience had left before the cops arrived on scene."

Augusta chuckled. "Here's how small this town is— Lenny is good friends with the Monroe County District Attorney, a man named Jim Marse. He's planning to talk to him today to see what he can find out."

Mal laughed. "Oh, you're in 'good-ole-boy' territory, are you? Well, that's a valuable connection for Evan, to have a new friend who is chummy with the local D.A."

Augusta recognized the change in his voice as he went into what she thought of as 'full detective mode.' "Gus, I have to ask this: How sure are you that Evan is innocent? Unless it's proven otherwise, he might have had opportunity. He definitely could have had motive."

"Evan did not murder Joan Cromer. I am absolutely positive."

"You said she was pushing him hard."

"Yes, she was. But Malcolm, he managed to control himself. They had an angry exchange of words, but he never threatened her physically. She continued to try to clutch him, and he pulled her hands away. But he was careful to never hurt her. It almost seemed…"

"…that she wanted him to?"

"Yes. How did you know that?"

"It's part of the pattern with a woman suffering from erotomania, the kind of obsession Joan Cromer seems to have had. They will taunt and push boundaries just to get any kind of a reaction from the person they're harassing. And it's frequently a celebrity. Some of these women have personality disorders. Joan sounds like a textbook case: stalking Evan to establish an intimate relationship with him. It's unfortunate he spent that one weekend with her."

Augusta felt a chill run across her shoulders and down her spine. "If you'd seen them…seen her in action…that was exactly how she was acting. But Evan didn't kill her, Mal. He's not capable of killing anyone, no matter how hard he might be pushed."

"He comes from a coal mining family, Gus. Miners are tough people."

"Evan is different. Yes, when he was a kid, he defended himself from bullies who went after him because he wanted to be a professional singer. He told me about that, and said he hated whenever it happened, but he had to stand up for himself. But it really went against his nature."

Malcolm didn't respond right away.

"Mal?"

"You're telling me he's a lover, not a fighter," he said slowly.

Augusta hesitated for a moment. "Well—yes. It seems to me there's a part of Evan that felt sorry for Joan, even though she was driving him to distraction. He would never have physically harmed her."

Back to Detective Mitchell mode. "Do you have any idea where she was staying?"

"Lenny plans to find that out when he talks to the D.A."

"I'll call you back tonight, after your show. Is Evan performing?"

66

"He has to. I think he needs to, as well. Yes, he has an understudy…but we all agree it's important for him to continue with the show."

"I concur. Well, I'll get there as soon as I can. Oh, and Gus?"

"Yes?"

Another change in Malcolm's tone of voice. "I've been listening to a recording of *Carousel*. I enjoyed the show when you directed it last year. Beautiful music. I'm looking forward to seeing you on stage."

"It's a good cast. Evan is perfect for Billy. I'm having a great time…well, I was."

Now Mal sounded closer to the mouthpiece, his voice low and intimate. "I've been listening to other songs you love as well. French songs. Duparc's 'Extase.'"

"Yes, I know you love that song." Augusta lowered her voice to match his. "We both remember the first time I sang it to you."

"Will you sing it for me when I get there?"

"Absolutely," she purred. "With only you to hear it."

"That's what I hoped you'd say."

Susan Moore Jordan

Chapter 5
The Loner

Just as Augusta hung up the phone, Len, Milly, and Evan returned from their hike to Buck Hill Falls. Evan sank onto the couch without saying a word and picked up the copy of *The Pocono Record* Augusta had been reading.

Len and Milly headed into the kitchen, Milly proclaiming, "I think I'll make some fresh coffee." Len rolled his eyes at Evan and raised his eyebrows, motioning Augusta to follow them.

"Look, I know this is upsetting, but Evan isn't making much of an effort here," Len said in a low voice. Milly made noise with cups and spoons until Len closed the door to the kitchen.

"How do you mean?" Augusta asked.

"We're trying to help. He didn't say two words to us on this hike," Len replied.

Milly knocked a few more things around. "Was he always this stand-offish?"

Augusta, taken aback, wasn't sure what to say. "He talked to me at breakfast."

"Only because you were prying information out of him. I'll admit, I don't know how I'd react if I thought I might be suspected of murdering someone. But we can't help if he won't even talk to us." Milly wiped her hands on a kitchen towel.

"You have to remember it's been ten years since I've seen him," Augusta said slowly. "Things between us were much different then. He was struggling to perform a role he felt wasn't well suited to his talents."

"Let me guess. You helped him." Milly put her hands on her hips. "So, he performed better than expected, and covered himself with glory."

"Well, I'm not sure about that, but he did a fine job and the audiences loved him."

A tap at the door interrupted their conversation. Len opened it and Evan stepped into the room, newspaper in hand.

He glanced at each of them. "I'm not very good at this. I think I owe you an apology." He ran a hand across the back of his neck. "You've been more than kind to me. Bringing me here so I wouldn't be alone, going out of your way to try to distract me this morning."

No response from any of them. Evan pulled out a tall stool and perched on it at the kitchen island. "I've always had a hard time warming up to people. I know I have this public face but it's not something that comes easily—I have to work at it. I wish I could just say thank you when I need to. I should have said it last night and again this morning."

"I'm sure this situation is overwhelming, Evan," Augusta said, moving toward him and placing a sympathetic hand on his arm. "You don't need to say anything."

Evan gazed at her with the hint of a sad smile.

Milly said abruptly, "Who wants coffee?"

They all busied themselves with cups, spoons, and cream and sugar.

Milly hissed in Augusta's ear, "Why did you do that? You're enabling his bad behavior."

Augusta stared at her. *She's right. I'm defensive of him. I'm making excuses for his rudeness.*

Len hoisted himself up onto another stool and looked directly at Evan. "You were about to say?"

"I was about to say thank you. Augusta's right, this is overwhelming." Evan held up the newspaper. "My name isn't in this article, thank God. It basically just says a woman's body was found in the parking lot at Pocono Playhouse last night. But I'm probably more than a— what do they call it? 'A person of interest.' Who else did Joan know in the Poconos besides me? I have to believe I'm the only suspect for this murder right now."

He folded the paper and laid it on the table. "Here's one of the bad things about celebrity. I'm never sure who my real friends are. I tend to hold myself apart because of that. I wish I'd been more cautious with Joan. I should never have gotten involved with her, not even for one weekend."

Augusta started to speak but Milly elbowed her in the ribs to be quiet.

"I also know this," Evan sipped his coffee. "I trust Augusta's friendship. And I can't believe the two of you are going to bat for me. Or maybe I can, because that's the way true friends operate."

"Sounds like your life is complicated, Evan," Len said, beginning to thaw.

"It always has been, Lenny," Evan took another swallow of coffee. "Since I was a kid in Carbondale who wanted to sing opera. You can probably imagine how spectacularly that went over with my coal miner family and friends."

He finished his coffee and gripped the cup as he deliberately set it down. "I've been trying to make some sense of Joan's death since last night. And not doing very well."

Milly nodded. "Definitely a shock. Not something you can get past easily, Evan. What do you plan to do about tonight's performance?" She gazed at him steadily.

"I plan to go onstage and play the role of Billy Bigelow as best I can." He returned her gaze. "It's what I do, Milly. I don't think it's going to be easy, though."

"Is there anything we can do to help?" Augusta said, still smarting from Milly's admonishing elbow to her ribs.

"You're doing it," he smiled as he spoke. "I kind of feel like I have a team here." He stood. "Is there anywhere around here I could go to run?"

"Run?" Milly and Len asked in unison.

"Yeah. I run in Central Park when I'm in New York. Just run. Not competitive running. It's one way I stay in shape. I have shoes with me."

"East Stroudsburg State College has a track at their field house," Lenny offered. "I can drive you down there. How long do you need?"

"An hour would be great. Maybe a little longer. It would help. It's also how I clear my head. I'll change." He headed upstairs.

"Ladies?" Len asked. "I have a couple of errands I can take care of while Evan is on the track. Either of you want to come with?"

"Why don't you go, Milly?" Augusta rubbed her side. "I have some phone calls I promised Malcolm I'd make."

"Sorry I jabbed you in the ribs."

"I'm not. You're right. This is Evan's crisis to face. It's hardly something that can be fixed with a talk about vocal technique and character development."

"Maybe it can. Only a different kind of character development." Milly smiled wryly before growing more serious. "You can't hold his hand and walk him through this, Augusta."

"Is that what I've been doing?"

"It's what you want to do. It's the way you treat your voice students sometimes. You're very protective of them." She stood directly in front of Augusta, wagging a finger at her. "Evan is not your student. He's a famous man facing a big problem. A major life event. Maybe a life-shattering event. We can be there for him, but he has to deal with this on his own."

***

By the time the three of them returned from East Stroudsburg, Augusta had satisfactorily tracked down Joan Cromer and had the name, address, and phone number of the organization she had worked with. Augusta heard them talking and even laughing when they came into the house.

"I'm going to grab a shower, if that's okay," Evan said.

"Sure, have at it," Len responded. He turned to Augusta after Evan was out of earshot. "I managed to catch the D.A. in his office in the courthouse. For starters, no autopsy report as yet. The cops did search Joan Cromer's room at Skytop last night."

"No doubt." Augusta stood and moved to Len's desk, where she replaced the notepad she'd been using. "It was nice to hear the camaraderie when you three came into the house."

Len nodded. "Evan's an okay guy. He's been by himself most of his life, apparently. He does the celebrity persona well, but it seems difficult for him to let people get close."

"Anyway," Milly called from the kitchen as she started preparing lunch, "Len warned Evan he'd no doubt be seeing Trooper LaBar this afternoon. I think he's ready for it."

Augusta leaned in the doorway. "Want any help?"

"I got this," Milly replied. "Len's right. Evan seems to be a genuinely nice person. Scared out of his wits, I think. And I get the feeling he's a lonely man." She stared hard at Augusta. "Is he still hung up on you?"

"I don't think so. Not really." Augusta helped herself to half a sandwich. "He's always had plenty of female attention. I believe he's alone by choice. I'm not sure why."

"Is he gay?" Milly asked, just as Evan came through the kitchen door.

"No, he isn't," Evan laughed. "You can be assured of one thing, Milly. I like women." He wrapped an arm around her waist and squeezed. "Especially women who cook."

Lenny, who had followed Evan into the kitchen, slapped plates and cutlery onto the kitchen island. "That particular lady is taken, Evan. You'll meet her man later tonight."

"The famous Cincinnati lawyer? Augusta told me last night he's a great guy. Impressive in the courtroom."

The four of them took seats, helping themselves to sandwiches, tossed salad, and sliced fruit.

"Garrett is absolutely the best," Augusta confirmed. "And Milly learned last night he's licensed to practice in Pennsylvania, so he can step in immediately to represent you."

Evan glanced around the room, a smile warming his eyes. "I guess I do have a team. It sure helps."

Len left the room to answer the phone, and returned fairly quickly. "Trooper LaBar. He asked if he could stop by to see you in about an hour. I told him that would be fine."

Evan wiped his mouth with his napkin. "Just as you predicted. What do you think he wants?"

"I told you Jim—the D.A.—said they searched Joan Cromer's room at Skytop. Maybe they found something they have questions about." Len leaned forward, elbows on the island. "He won't be coming to arrest you, Evan. They're still investigating Joan's death, and at the moment the cause is 'undetermined.' Just be straightforward and give him honest answers."

"Got it." Evan replaced the half sandwich he had picked up. "Would all of you excuse me, please? Maybe sweats and a T-shirt aren't the best wardrobe choices for this upcoming scene."

Murmurs of assent as they heard him going back upstairs.

"I guess we should make ourselves scarce for this interview," Milly said. "Augusta, you met this cop last night…maybe you should answer the door."

Milly and Len left for their rooms as Augusta waited with Evan, now in slacks and a collared shirt open at the neck, for Trooper LaBar's arrival.

"How does this work?"

"He'll be professional and straightforward. Just tell him the truth. I imagine he'll ask me to leave the two of you alone."

To Augusta's surprise, Trooper LaBar didn't make that request, and the three of them sat down in the living room.

"Mr. Llewellyn, we found letters in Miss Cromer's room which appeared to be from you. Addressed to her in Cincinnati. Signed with your name."

After a moment of dumbfounded silence, Evan replied, "I didn't write them. I never wrote Miss

Cromer." He managed to maintain his calm. "We spent one weekend together in Indianapolis last year. She wrote me by way of my agent a couple of times. I never read anything beyond the first letter. I found that one a little alarming, frankly. Any additional correspondence I threw away. I didn't even open those letters."

"In what way did that letter alarm you?"

"Her memory of our weekend was nothing like mine. She claimed we were in love and I had all but proposed to her. Entirely untrue. The word 'love' never came up when we were together."

"I see." LaBar made another note. "Would you be willing to provide a sample of your handwriting?"

"Certainly, I'll be glad to do that. Trooper LaBar, I suggest you check the handwriting in those letters against Miss Cromer's. She obviously had some sort of obsession with me. She showed up in a couple of other cities where the tour stopped. When she attempted to approach me after the performance, I tried to ignore her. When she persisted, I took her aside and told her there was nothing between us and demanded she stop following me."

Evan's voice had begun to rise, and Augusta deliberately knocked a throw pillow to the floor. "Oh, I'm so sorry." She leaned forward to pick up the pillow, and saw by Evan's face he got the message.

He continued more calmly, "There was never any further involvement of any kind after that one weekend."

LaBar jotted notes on his pad. "Do you recall where Miss Cromer attempted to see you after that?"

"Yes. Rochester, New York. Atlanta, Georgia. If you'd like I can provide exact dates from the tour calendar. And more recently, at Lincoln Center in New York. I can give you those dates as well."

"That would be helpful." LaBar paused for a moment. "We also found an appointment book in her room, with your name and the names of resorts on certain dates. It appeared she had been with you, or expected to be with you, on those dates at those locations."

Evan stared at Trooper LaBar. "Unbelievable. Another figment of this—crazy woman's imagination." His voice rose again.

"You have to realize how distressing this is for Mr. Llewellyn," Augusta said hastily.

"None of that is true," Evan said, regaining his air of calm. "Any 'romance' existed strictly in her head. I can't tell you how much I regret having spent that one weekend with her."

"We can check with those venues to see what they recall of her visits."

Augusta noted the trooper's noncommittal response to what he had just heard. *A true professional*, she thought. The kind of interview she had witnessed Malcolm give.

"You don't have her address or phone number?"

"No. I told you the few letters I received from her I destroyed." Evan managed to keep his voice under control. "She had some kind of mental condition, in my opinion."

"Do you know anything else about her?"

"Not much, other than she told me that she worked as an event planner in Cincinnati. I know I'm repeating myself, but I made it very clear our weekend together was strictly casual."

"That kind of unwanted attention must have been difficult for you. Frustrating. Maybe maddening, if she continued to insist there was a romance between you."

Careful how you answer that. Augusta watched as Evan thought for a moment before replying.

"It was all of that, because she refused to listen to me. When she spoke with me at the after party on Monday night, I threatened to take some kind of legal action if she didn't leave me the hell alone." He motioned toward Augusta. "Mrs. Mitchell witnessed that discussion."

LaBar looked at Augusta with renewed interest. "Is that so? Would you be willing to provide us with information about what you witnessed in that confrontation?"

"I believe Mr. Llewellyn referred to it as a discussion, Trooper LaBar. Yes, certainly." *Surely he can't believe I would incriminate Evan,* Augusta thought.

"Well, I believe that covers everything for now." LaBar handed Evan a piece of paper. "I wonder if you wouldn't mind copying this paragraph from one of the letters so we can verify it isn't your handwriting?"

Evan stood. "If you'll excuse me for a moment, Trooper LaBar, I need to get my glasses."

LaBar nodded. "Certainly."

"I'll get a pen and some paper," Augusta offered, noticing that the paper in LaBar's hand had been typed. *Of course. They don't want him to see the handwriting on the original.*

Providing the sample was accomplished quickly, and Trooper LaBar took his leave of them. Evan took a deep breath once the trooper had left the house and they heard his car pull away.

"Can you believe she wrote herself letters and pretended they were from me?" He shook his head in disbelief as he folded his glasses and replaced them in their case. "Well, that wasn't too awful. He seems like a reasonable guy."

"Don't let your guard down," Augusta sternly reminded Evan. "Don't forget, Len told us they don't have the autopsy report yet, so Joan isn't officially a murder victim and that was a preliminary interview—a fishing expedition. You handled yourself well. I doubt you'll hear anything more before tomorrow."

"So I guess...I need to get my head into Billy Bigelow and *Carousel* for tonight's performance." He stood and moved slowly to the window. "Did I ever tell you I had a lot of problems learning to read? I finally had a great teacher in sixth grade who had my eyes tested. For starters, I'm farsighted. I need glasses to read. I also learned I'm dyslexic."

"No, you never mentioned it. You had a reputation for being a quick study. It's amazing you overcame it to that extent."

"Not without a struggle." Evan stared out of the window for a long moment. "Another reason I didn't fit

80

in as a kid. 'Four-eyes Evan.' All the way through high school."

"You never told me about that. You did tell me about defending yourself when someone tried to pick a fight."

"My cousin Rhys taught me how to fight. He's two years older than me. There were times when it was us two against three or four." Evan turned back toward Augusta.

"Growing up in Carbondale wasn't easy, Augusta. I like playing Billy. I can relate to him pretty damn well, you know." He grinned wryly. "I have an idea Billy Bigelow had a tough time as a kid, too. You know, he really loved Julie. I mean, I think he would have died for her."

"But instead, he hit her."

"Yes…but you see, he didn't know how to talk to her. Julie was smart, and that scared him. And when Billy got scared, he wanted to smash things. He couldn't sort out his fear from his anger." He paused, thinking. "Emily and I have talked about this part—Billy didn't understand how to respond to love. Either someone loving him or the feelings of love he began to feel with Julie."

"What are you—Evan Llewellyn—feeling at this moment?"

"Scared and angry. And sad. Scared that I may be arrested for murder. Angry that Joan caused all this. And despite that, sad that somebody murdered her. Nobody deserves that."

Augusta started to say something, but Evan lifted a hand to stop her. "I know what you're going to say, 'use those feelings tonight in your performance.' That's exactly what I intend to do."

Chapter 6
Billy Bigelow and Julie Jordan

Thursday 4:00 p.m.

Augusta called Malcolm after Evan's meeting with
Trooper LaBar and passed on what she'd learned that
day, including the name of the organization Joan Cromer
worked for in Cincinnati. She also told him about Evan's
meeting with the lead investigator. Mal agreed Evan had
handled himself well.

"Won't Garrett get to look at the appointment book
the police found? And the letters presumably written by
Evan?" Augusta asked Malcolm.

"Absolutely. All evidence must be shared with the
defense attorney." He paused. "You sound as if you
believe Evan will be arrested."

"You said it yourself, Joan Cromer's behavior was
so bizarre and distressing it could be construed as
motive. He's strong enough to have strangled her.
Opportunity—that remains to be determined. But if Evan

was in his dressing room that entire fifteen to twenty minutes and no one was with him...."

"Is that his account of what happened?" Mal asked.

"Unfortunately, it is. He had a headache and took the opportunity to swallow a couple of aspirin and close his eyes. He asked the assistant stage manager to call him five minutes before his entrance."

Mal remained quiet for a moment. "Jim and I plan to stop at the Cromers' sometime tomorrow. Not exactly an official call. I want to tell them you met Joan briefly and asked me to extend your condolences. Mrs. Cromer might be more relaxed under those circumstances. Is that okay with you?"

"Not entirely true, but if you need it, use it." She sighed. "Here's one thing that concerns me...a lot. Joan Cromer was visiting here and it doesn't seem she knew a soul other than Evan. So where do the state police look for other suspects? Right now, Evan is the only person they have. I can't tell you how much I hate this."

"Understood. Having someone you care about as a suspect in a murder can be frightening. Take some deep breaths, Augusta. This is a whole new experience for you."

"I just wish there were something I could do." Her voice quivered. "I feel so helpless."

"You're doing everything you can. Evan's lucky you were there when this happened. Garrett will be there soon. Let him take the lead."

"I understand what you're telling me. Don't try to play cop." She laughed shakily.

"You're used to being in charge, Gus. But this is completely out of your hands. When I get there I'll find some way to meet with Trooper LaBar. Then I'll have a better sense of what's going on. In the meantime, immerse yourself in the show. I'll bet that's what you're telling Evan."

"You do know me, don't you?" Another shaky chuckle. "I love you so much, Mal."

"I love you, too, Gus. More than I can ever tell you."

***

Garrett's plane was due into Newark Airport at 6:30 p.m., so Len and Milly left at 4:00 to give themselves plenty of time, taking a basket of snacks and a thermos of coffee with them. They expected to be back at Lenny's home at Buck Hill no later than 9:30. Milly and Augusta had put lasagna together for a late supper for all of them to enjoy once the actors returned from the theater. Augusta and Evan raided the refrigerator for snacks before they left the house.

Evan sat quietly on the drive to the Playhouse.

"Penny for your thoughts?"

He sighed. "Just wondering how the audience will receive me tonight. How the cast members will feel about me. I have to wonder what kind of gossip has been floating around."

"I very much doubt any of the people in the audience will have heard a thing beyond the body of a woman having been found last night. Your name wasn't in the paper. There's nothing to connect you to her."

"It's a small town, Augusta. People talk. Who knows what might be floating around?"

"The cast will be fine. You know how theater people close ranks."

Their car was one of the first in the parking lot, but the few people who were already in the theater went out of their way to speak to Evan.

"Hey, Evan. I put water in your dressing room. Let me know if you need more, will ya?" ..."Hey, Billy Bigelow! You're the man!"... "Evan, I've already collected your props for you."

Augusta grinned at her friend. "As I was just saying...."

She saw the crinkle around his eyes as he smiled in return. "Yes, you were."

They were to play to a full house, and prior to the performance Augusta was aware of heightened pre-show chatter. *Maybe there is talk around town. It's possible other people recalled seeing Evan with someone briefly during the after party on Monday night. Or someone may have seen Joan on Tuesday night when she tried to speak to him after the show.*

The opening number in the show *Carousel* is a pantomime to Richard Rodgers' "Carousel Waltz." The music of the waltz was a great favorite of Augusta's—a well-constructed, beautiful piece of music, painting in sound the movement of the carousel. For this production the director had included every cast member in the pantomime, even if for only a few moments. As Nettie, Augusta took the two children in the cast onstage and helped Evan as Billy, the carousel barker, gives them about a two-minute ride on the two-horse carousel.

Their eyes met and Augusta saw that Evan's were shining. *He's really on tonight.* Two women in the ensemble took charge of the kids and Augusta stood in the wings to enjoy the music and watch the rest of the pantomime scene. Near the end Billy lifted Emily, in the role of Julie Jordan, onto a horse, and locked eyes with her as he turned the carousel until the curtains closed.

They were a strikingly attractive couple—Evan's classic good looks, accentuated by his startlingly light gray eyes; Emily's large, expressive brown eyes and wavy dark hair, cascading below her shoulders. Evan helped Emily from the carousel horse and lightly brushed her cheek with his lips, a move that hadn't been part of the staging. The audience didn't see it since his back was to them. *Hmm, where did that come from?*

Augusta stayed backstage to watch as the performance continued, including the extended "bench scene," a long, romantic sequence between Billy and Julie, more music than dialogue. Each character sang the well-loved piece "If I Loved You," ending with the couple in an embrace. The kiss continued after the curtains closed. *Evan, what are you doing?*

The next scene included one of Augusta's big vocal numbers, "June Is Bustin' Out All Over." She put Evan out of her mind and immersed herself in the role and the music she so enjoyed. The entire cast seemed to be performing at a higher level, and it felt exciting to be part of that.

Near the end of the act Evan sang the "Soliloquy." Milly had been right to label it an aria. Billy Bigelow has just learned Julie, now his wife, is carrying his child. His first reaction is excitement about having a son to share the things he loves with. But then his thoughts turn to the possibility his child might be a girl, who will need more than his love—she'll need to be provided for. And Billy at the moment has no job and no prospects. The end of the aria expresses his desperation to provide for her in any way he can, coming up with the money he'll need by any means possible. Evan stopped the show with his intense, passionate performance.

A brief reprise of "June Is Bustin' Out All Over" brought the act to a close.

Miles caught Augusta during intermission before she could go to her dressing room. "I wasn't sure I should say anything to Evan. Trooper LaBar was here today and asked me again about exactly where Evan was during the first act last night. I'm not sure how, but he knew about that stretch when Billy isn't onstage. I assumed Evan was in his dressing room but I don't know how that could be confirmed."

"Evan told me he took a couple of aspirin and went into his dressing room to close his eyes. The assistant stage manager gave him a five-minute call. So, he was alone for most of that time."

Miles stared at his feet. "Time is strange, isn't it? Twenty minutes can be long enough for something awful to happen. Or far too short to fight off a headache."

"Still, I don't see how he could have left the theater, gone out to the parking lot, had an…altercation…with a woman, come back inside and gone onstage in twenty minutes."

Miles shook his head. "I can't either. But don't be surprised if the cops decide to time it."

"I can't believe we're standing backstage in the middle of a show talking calmly about how long it takes to choke someone to death." Augusta's eyes widened.

"I already asked a friend about that. It can happen pretty quickly. Sometimes in just a couple of minutes."

Augusta couldn't resist. "Was he speaking from experience? Was he the strang-*ler* or the strang-*lee*?" They both had to laugh.

"God, this is awful," Miles ruefully shook his head. "Let's try to stay in *Carousel*, can we? It's bad enough that Billy falls on his knife and dies in order to avoid going to jail."

The assistant stage manager was already giving the five-minute warning and Augusta ran to her dressing room to powder her face and neck. *And the show goes on*, she thought.

She had a few incidental solos in the opening number of Act Two, then in the second scene performed "You'll Never Walk Alone"…singing it to Evan, who lay on the stage floor as Billy until he was raised up by the Heavenly Starkeeper to begin his journey to the afterlife.

Augusta stayed in the wings to hear Evan sing "The Highest Judge of All" and was moved by his fine performance, fully aware that the words had new meaning for him. Emily stood next to her. Augusta realized Emily was crying and put her arms around the young woman.

"I'm so scared for him, Augusta," Emily sobbed softly. "He told me he thinks Joan Cromer was murdered and that the police may believe he did it."

"You and I, and a lot of other people, know better. Keep the faith." *She's in love with him. Maybe he has decided to explore what might be between them. She's a lovely young woman, and he's...well, at the moment, he's a murder suspect. But he's certainly a man who needs love.*

The performance ended with another standing ovation, and after a brief meet and greet between the actors and audience members, Augusta and Evan headed back to Len's.

"Terrific performance, Evan. I mean that. I've never heard 'The Highest Judge of All' sung as well as you sang it tonight."

"Thanks. Wasn't Emily lovely? The 'bench scene' really clicked. And when she said her goodbye after I killed myself, she made me cry." He grinned at her. "Then you sang the hell out of 'You'll Never Walk Alone' and I was a soggy mess. I'm surprised I could even get through 'The Highest Judge,' frankly."

"Yes, it was definitely an emotional performance," Augusta chuckled. "Evan...about Emily...."

"You saw the kiss onstage?" He shook his head ruefully. "Shouldn't have happened. I can't get caught up in what's going on with me and turn to her to make me feel better. She doesn't deserve that."

"And you just proved what I knew, that you're better than that. Accept her friendship. When this is over, rethink what you might have with her."

Augusta signaled for her turn off of the main highway. "I like Emily. I know she's young. She's also smart, perceptive, and level-headed. Sometimes May-December matches work out well."

Evan sat up straight and turned toward her. "May-*December*? Come on, Augusta. I'm not *that* old. May-*September*."

"You are ever-youthful and look about thirty. Emily's twenty-four, but when she piles that gorgeous hair on top of her head she could pass for twenty-eight, so you're only two years older than she is."

By the end of this exchange, they were both laughing.

"Is that how you worked around your age difference with the detective?" Evan snorted.

"No, he told me he's way older than I am in life experience," Augusta giggled. "I liked that."

They were still laughing as she pulled up into Len's driveway. "Back to reality," Augusta said.

They sat quietly for a moment and Evan commented, "Yes. I get to meet the famous Garrett Stoddard. Well, we put on one hell of a show tonight. Hopefully, those will continue."

The wonderful aroma of lasagna greeted them as they entered the house. Garrett commandeered his client for a casual, friendly conversation, which Augusta knew delved much deeper than Evan suspected.

Over coffee, Len introduced new information. "I had a phone call from the D.A. tonight, just minutes after we walked in the door from the airport. Three things: first, the autopsy report confirms that Joan Cromer was strangled. Time of death is set between eight and ten last night. Since audience members were arriving as late as eight-fifteen, she was no doubt killed after the performance of *Carousel* had started."

Silence from his listeners. Len glanced around at them. "It gets worse, I'm afraid. You know that box in the paper this morning asking for any potential witnesses to come forward? A couple showed up at the Mt. Pocono barracks of the State Police, where the Investigative Unit is stationed."

Garrett picked up the narration, using his best courtroom manner. "These people had arrived late for the show, and ran inside after they parked. But they noticed a man and woman in another part of the lot having what appeared to be an out-of-control argument."

He stood, presenting the case. "They were at a distance, and the lighting was poor, but they agreed to look at a photo array to see if they could identify the man."

I know what's coming, thought Augusta, her hands going cold.

Garrett moved to stand directly in front of Evan.

"Unfortunately, they selected your photo."

Chapter 7
The Suspect

"Where the hell did they get my picture?" Evan demanded.

"From the playbill. They enlarged and enhanced it," Len told him.

Augusta said quickly, "That can't possibly be a valid identification. From what you just told us, the witnesses barely glanced at the man and woman before running into the theater. The lighting in that lot is dreadful. You said they weren't even close to the people they saw."

"It's a questionable ID," Garrett agreed. "And eyewitnesses can be unreliable. But there's one more thing we learned from D.A. Marse."

Garrett was at his finest when addressing a jury, and he used those skills with his listeners. "It's been determined that Evan's whereabouts during a part of the performance are unknown. For a period of time long enough for him to have left the theater, strangled the victim, and returned to make his next entrance, no one backstage can confirm where he was."

He pushed his chair back. "It's a weak case. But it might be enough to make an arrest."

Augusta noted that the blood had drained from Evan's face.

"And then I go to jail."

"Actually, I don't believe you will," Garrett said. "The evidence is all circumstantial. It happens more than you realize that the first person arrested for a crime turns out to be innocent—but under these circumstances, there's a lot of pressure on the cops to arrest *somebody*."

He thought for a moment. "Here's what I believe will happen next. You'll be asked to come to the state police barracks for additional questioning. I'll go with you and point out the problems with their case, if I need to. Chances are instead of arresting you, they'll make it clear you're a suspect in an ongoing murder investigation and advise you not to leave town."

"This is unreal." Evan ran a hand through his hair. "I swear to God, I wish I had never laid eyes on Joan Cromer."

"In the meantime, the Pennsylvania State Police won't stop investigating the case," Garrett told them. "I think they realize they don't have enough to charge you at the moment. And again, it's all circumstantial except that one eyewitness identification, which we agree is questionable. Here's what they are dealing with: a visitor to their jurisdiction was brutally murdered. They want to find her killer. Anybody have any ideas?" His glance swept the room. "I didn't think so."

Milly stood. "It's almost two o'clock, people. Let's try to get some sleep and start digging into this tomorrow, shall we? It won't hurt to start building our case now but keep in mind that one of the best detectives in the world will be here in a few days, and dollars to donuts he'll figure out the real killer."

Augusta had a momentary image of Malcolm in a coat of shining armor, seated on a white horse. *He'd like that. My hero cop. Sir Knight Mitchell to the rescue.*

"Agreed," Garrett pronounced. He shook an index finger in Evan's face. "I'm sure sleep is out of the question for you. Make some notes. Write down as much as you can recall about every single thing Joan Cromer said to you while you were together. It's surprising what people come up with when they really give their memory banks a workout."

Augusta helped Len wash and put away the supper dishes. "You know that's problematic, don't you?" He asked her. "About Malcolm coming in and solving the case."

"I'm sure the Pennsylvania State Police won't look kindly on any outside interference. But they'd be foolish not to accept his help."

"It's their case, Augusta. He has to tread carefully. When's he getting here, anyway?"

She sighed. "Probably not until Monday evening. Darn it."

***

As Garrett had predicted, Evan was contacted the next morning and asked to come to Mt. Pocono as soon as possible to talk to the PSP investigators. He was driven to his interview by a small army of supporters. With Evan's permission, Augusta had phoned Emily and asked her to come with them. Garrett's thought was the more, the better—an obvious show of support for a suspect many people were sure was innocent. Miles joined them to represent the Playhouse.

Garrett of course had brought all necessary paperwork indicating his status of board approval to practice law in the Commonwealth of Pennsylvania. As Evan's attorney he was permitted to enter the barracks with his client. The others parked across the street and waited.

It was a warm day, and they were all grateful for a fairly stiff breeze. They glanced around and Augusta remarked, "Mt. Pocono is picturesque, but I see that four-lane highway and wonder if it might someday be overrun with traffic. I guess it's progress, but it's kind of sad."

"I remember Stroudsburg as a charming old town. Is it still the same?" Milly asked.

"Stroudsburg is actually much the same, for the most part. It still has tree-lined streets. We should drive down there and stroll through downtown. Maybe wander through Wyckoff's."

"What's that? A local store?" Emily asked.

"An especially nice department store. You'll like it." Augusta assured her. "Oh, and there's a lovely boutique on Main Street, too—Frances Burrough's. You'll both love that."

"Clothes shopping? What fun." Emily turned to Augusta. "You know, I'd love to shop with you sometime. You always look so perfectly put together—so stylish."

"I have to admit, clothes are a passion of mine, And shoes in particular." She laughed. "Once in a while my husband even comes along on one of my shopping excursions."

Garrett and Evan emerged forty-five minutes later, crossed the street and rejoined their small army, which waited expectantly for the news. Evan draped an arm around Emily's shoulders and she gazed up at him, her arm around his waist.

"Well, they definitely look good together," Milly murmured in Augusta's ear.

As if on cue, a car pulled up further down the block and out jumped a photographer. Len headed him off, asking if he'd wait for permission from Mr. Llewellyn's attorney before taking any pictures. In the meantime, everyone who had accompanied Evan loaded themselves quickly into their cars, but not before *The Pocono Record* staffer managed to get a couple of photos.

"So much for trying to keep this quiet," Augusta commented to Milly, seated next to her, with Evan and Emily in the back. "Hold on, folks." She pulled away from the curb with an impressive squeal of tires, causing them all to laugh.

"No, it's okay," Evan said. "This had to happen. How many murders have taken place at the Pocono Playhouse...ever? I know I'm innocent. All of you know I'm innocent."

"Where to, boss?" Augusta asked Milly.

"Well, I have lunch all ready at the house. We just need to set it out. Can we keep that photographer, reporter…whatever he is…off private property?"

By this time, several other cars had fallen in behind them, in addition to the newsperson from the *Record* and the two cars containing the rest of Evan's entourage.

"Some excitement for the folks in Monroe County," Augusta chortled. "Hang on, guys. We're taking the long way home." She headed down Route 611, and once they had exited the borough of Mt. Pocono her foot pressed down on the accelerator.

While it's true the Poconos are more tall hills than real mountains, there are plenty of back roads that wind and dip. Augusta had a great time resurrecting her driving skills, much to Milly's consternation.

"Augusta! What the hell are you doing? Who taught you to drive like this?" Milly clutched her lap belt and the dashboard alternately.

"Uncle Lenny. Who else?" Augusta made a swerve and a sharp left turn. Evan and Emily laughed as they clutched each other, enjoying the ride.

Remarkably, all of the cars stayed with her, but when they finally pulled up at Len's house the *Record* staff member backed up, turned around, and drove away.

"Under orders from his boss, I'd bet," Augusta said.

Len's was the last car in the driveway, with Garrett as his passenger. Milly started counting heads for lunch: the four in their car, Len and Garrett, Miles in his own car.

"Only seven? Darn, we should have invited the reporter and a couple of state cops. There's a ton of food."

***

"George LaBar. Nice guy, impressive member of the Pennsylvania State Police," Garrett commented as all of them sat down to enjoy Milly's lunch. "They've earned their reputation. He didn't say as much, but I have the feeling he's hoping to find another suspect for Joan Cromer's murder."

"It was great to have my attorney with me," Evan grinned. "Garrett did most of the talking."

"That's why I was there, to speak in my client's behalf. The PSP is aware they don't yet have enough of a case to arrest Evan, eyewitnesses or not. It was a help to me that Trooper LaBar was agreeable to making copies of the items they found in Miss Cromer's room at the resort for me to look over."

Evan added, "So basically, Trooper LaBar repeated what he's been saying since Wednesday night, for me not to leave town while the investigation into Joan's murder is continuing."

After lunch, Miles took his leave of them. Milly assigned clean up duty to Evan and Emily, while Garrett and Augusta commandeered the library to work on the case.

Garrett had requested and been given a copy of the appointment book that had been discovered in Joan's room at Skytop, and under his direction Augusta made

99

calls to each of the resorts where Joan had indicated a supposed meeting with Evan. Garrett wrote busily, stopping occasionally when Augusta gave him a report from each of the six resorts she called.

"Well, the same result each time. Yes, she had been there, but the reservation was in her name only, and none of the people at the desk recalled seeing a male companion with her." Augusta stood and stretched.

"Confirming what Evan told us. These were all figments of Joan's overactive imagination."

"Any result from the handwriting expert?"

"No, we won't have that until Monday. I'm sure we'll find Evan was truthful about that as well." Garrett stood and moved around the room. "My guess is Joan Cromer may have suffered from a condition known as erotomania, where the object of the fixation is nearly always a celebrity."

"Does Evan have..." Augusta corrected herself. "*Did* he have any legal recourse at all against her harassment?"

"Not really. Only if she had broken into his hotel room or perhaps a theater dressing room and stolen something. Did he say anything about that?"

"No. But I'm sure you'll ask him."

Garrett resumed his seat, picking up the legal pad he'd been writing on. "At this point I need to talk with my client."

He tapped his teeth with his pen. "What's going on between him and Emily? She's lovely, by the way. And young."

Augusta snorted. "She's both, but she's also a bright young woman. Right now, a growing friendship. She'd like it to be more, but I think Evan intends to keep his head about that. He doesn't want to hurt her. That might change once this is over. There's definitely chemistry between them."

Garrett smiled. "It's good that he's being careful. I'd prefer to see him in private. Or rather, I'd like you here to make notes. I think he would be comfortable with that."

"I'll ask Milly and Len to drive Emily back to the cast house. Evan actually picked her up there this morning."

When Evan joined them in the library, he had the notes he'd made the night before that Garrett had requested. Augusta had already heard most of what he had to say, that this all started with that weekend in Indianapolis.

"Joan was a damned attractive woman and I...well, I enjoyed our time together. She was funny and charming. I made it clear that for me this could only be a casual liaison. I was led to believe she accepted that and it was all she expected or wanted, as well."

Evan went on to tell Garrett about Joan approaching him during the following months, first in Rochester, New York, and then again in Atlanta. He said he had barely spoken to her either time.

"Did you discover some personal item missing after that weekend in Indianapolis?"

Evan gave it some thought. "Trooper LaBar asked me the same thing Wednesday night—no, Thursday morning. And I don't remember anything. I honestly thought that was the end of Joan pursuing me." He ran a hand across the back of his neck. "It was several months later that she showed up in New York in March. I couldn't believe it."

"And then she came here."

"She did. I didn't realize she was here until opening night of *Carousel* when she approached me at the after party."

Augusta and Evan both described that encounter as Garrett continued to make copious notes.

"You saw her Tuesday night?"

"I avoided her Tuesday night. She was standing near my car when I left the theater. I gave her what I hoped was a murderous look, got in my car and drove away."

"Careful about using words like 'murderous' when you talk to the cops," Garrett said mildly.

"Well, after Monday...I just wanted her gone."

"Another phrase I would avoid."

Garrett studied his notes again. "She told you she was an event planner from Cincinnati, and that she had graduated from Withrow High School. Did she say anything else about herself? Likes, dislikes? The smallest detail might be helpful."

"She told me she didn't care for opera. She liked movies, especially romantic musicals. She was most attracted to men with blue or gray eyes. She preferred wine to liquor."

He flushed. "She...liked my body. She talked about that a lot."

"You didn't see her at all on Wednesday night?"

"Not until Trooper LaBar took us…Augusta and me…to identify her remains."

"And now we've learned no one can confirm your claim that you were in your dressing room during that period of time you were not onstage during Act One."

"The assistant stage manager can confirm I was in my room when she gave me a five-minute warning for my next entrance, as I asked her to." He glanced down. "But I was alone in my dressing room for a quarter of an hour. Give or take a couple of minutes."

"To the best of your knowledge, Miss Cromer didn't know anyone here in the Poconos?"

"She never mentioned knowing anyone."

Garrett flipped the pad closed. "I think that covers it, Evan. The prosecution has a very weak case against you, hinging primarily on a questionable eyewitness identification and fifteen minutes you can't account for. Augusta and I just checked on those supposed 'dates' in Miss Cromer's address book and learned she checked in by herself at each of those hotels. I'm sure the handwriting sample will prove you did not write the letters that were found."

He stood. "The Pennsylvania State Police are continuing to investigate Joan Cromer's murder. Let's hope they come up with another suspect soon."

Evan leaned forward, propping his chin on his hand. "So now I have to go to the theater tonight and perform again."

"Is that a bad thing? Augusta tells me you were exceptional last night." Garrett smiled grimly. "One thing for sure, you'll have sold out houses for the rest of your run here."

***

Miles met Augusta and Evan outside the theater, folded newspaper in hand. "I figured you might as well see this now, so you'll have some time to…well, to get used to it, I guess. The first time…or at least one of the few times *The Pocono Record* has ever issued a special edition."

Evan took the paper, staring at the headline:

STAGE PERFORMER EVAN LLEWELLYN QUESTIONED IN MURDER OF WOMAN AT POCONO PLAYHOUSE

Two large photos of Evan, one with Garrett preceding him as he exited the PSP barracks, the other of him getting into Augusta's car. Evan skimmed the short article under the photos and handed the paper to Augusta.

Friday, June 10, 4:00 p.m.—Popular matinee idol and opera singer Evan Llewellyn, appearing currently in the role of Billy Bigelow in the Pocono Playhouse production of *Carousel*, was questioned earlier today about the murder of Joan Cromer, 35, of Cincinnati, Ohio. Cromer's lifeless body was discovered on Wednesday night in the parking lot of the Playhouse. According to the Pennsylvania State Police investigation, an autopsy indicated Miss Cromer died as the result of strangulation sometime between 8 and 10 p.m. on June 8. Two witnesses told police they arrived late to the theater and saw an altercation in the parking lot between Miss Cromer and a man they identified as Mr. Llewellyn.

Miss Cromer was a guest at Skytop Lodge and had checked in on Monday afternoon, June 6. The PSP has notified her family in Cincinnati of her death.

Llewellyn is being represented by Garrett Stoddard, a defense attorney from Cincinnati who arrived in Pennsylvania late Thursday night. Mr. Stoddard responded to questions about the case with a declaration that the investigation is ongoing and he believes the PSP will find the person responsible for Miss Cromer's death soon.

Mrs. Rowena Stevens, founder and owner of the Playhouse, expressed her utmost confidence in Mr. Llewellyn's innocence and said he will fulfill his obligation to the Playhouse and complete the run of *Carousel*.

"This was a terrible thing to have happen right outside our Playhouse. Mr. Llewellyn is a beloved performer who is wrongly suspected of committing this crime. I am sure the Pennsylvania State Police will quickly find the killer and bring him to justice. In the meantime, we will support Mr. Llewellyn one hundred percent."

Augusta finished reading the article and wordlessly returned the paper to Miles. She turned to Evan and was stunned to see his reaction. Eyes flashing, he took a deep breath, pulled himself up to his full height, and clenched his fists. "All I have to say is if Rowena is supporting me one hundred percent, she's going to get the best damn performance of Billy Bigelow she's ever seen. Somebody set me up for this murder. Augusta, get your detective up here pronto to find out who did this." He strode into the theater, leaving Augusta and Miles staring open-mouthed after him.

Miles followed quickly. "I need to calm him down a little. No scenery chewing." He rubbed his hands gleefully. "But, man…this is going to be some show."

Evan's words rang in Augusta's ears: *'Somebody set me up for this murder.'*

Certainly possible. But who? And why? Not to mention, how?

Chapter 8
Meanwhile, back in Cincinnati...

Cincinnati
Saturday, June 11
9:30 a.m.

"And then...," Malcolm prompted.

"Then Evan pulled the cast together before we started the performance. He told them exactly what was going on, including how angry and scared he is. And just as you'd expect, they closed ranks around him. Sometimes he can be reserved, even stand-offish, but he broke all that down last night and the troops rallied. We put on quite a show. The audience gave us a lengthy standing ovation, and a lot of them were in tears. It was definitely a thrill."

"Sounds like quite an experience, Gus."

"It absolutely was that." She laughed. "It will be tough to get to that level again tonight, but I won't be surprised if it happens. I think it kind of shocked Evan to realize how much people care about him."

"Thanks for catching me up on what's happened with the case. It's good that Garrett is there."

"It sure is. He doesn't think much will happen over the weekend, unless the state police have more leads. That's tricky, though, since Joan Cromer was visiting the area and so far as we are aware, she didn't know anyone here except Evan. I would guess that's what they're working on."

"Well, the case made *The Morning Call* today. Including a mention that you're part of the cast."

"Oh, great. I expect you may hear from our favorite Cincinnati reporter, Arnold Richter."

"Entirely possible." Neither of them was fond of Richter, but at times in the past he had been a useful contact.

Malcolm glanced at his watch. "Jim and I are headed for the Cromer's as soon as he gets here. I'll let you know everything I find out."

"Any chance of you getting here sooner than Monday night?" Malcolm heard the yearning in her voice. *Hang in there, Gus.*

"Not much, I'm afraid. The Michelson case has been handed to the jury, and I don't expect I'll be needed again, but you never know until the verdict is in."

A pause, and then Augusta's voice close and warm in his ear. "I can't believe how much I miss you."

"Yeah, me, too. This sounds sappy, but I've been sleeping on your pillow."

"Not sappy. Wonderfully romantic. Well, just two more nights, my love."

"Don't expect to get much sleep Monday night."

She chuckled. "I'm counting on that."

Mal sighed as he hung up the phone, rubbing Fritz's warm, soft head and patting his flanks as the dog whined softly. "Yeah, you miss her, too, don't you, buddy? Well, you'll be spending some time with Caruso soon. I know you're going to love that."

He gave the dog a treat and closed the door between the living room and the alcove, making sure Fritz had plenty of chew toys lying around in the back part of the house. The television set in the alcove was tuned to cartoons. Malcolm shook his head and grinned. *What a spoiled pup. Well, he's worth it.*

"See you later, Fritz," Malcolm said, watching his dog's ears droop as he realized his master was leaving the house. "Oh, stop. You're fine."

Mal loped down the front walk and jumped in his partner Jim Edmond's car.

"Let me guess. You left Fritz with chew toys and the TV playing cartoons, right?"

"Yeah. You know me too well," Malcolm laughed.

Jim gave Malcolm a sidelong glance. "Sorry you agreed to Augusta going to Pennsylvania for these two weeks?"

"No, not really. It's probably a good thing she was there when all hell broke loose."

"For sure. And now Garrett Stoddard is on the scene, correct?"

"He is. He flew up Thursday, the day after Joan Cromer's body was discovered. The police have interviewed Evan Llewellyn twice, but they haven't charged him…yet. Gus says Garrett doesn't think they have much of a case and he's sure they must be looking for other suspects. Though that's tough, since Joan is from out of town and doesn't seem to have any contacts in the Poconos."

"Well, maybe that will change after we talk to her parents." Jim turned right onto Erie Avenue. "Kind of interesting that the Cromers are practically neighbors of yours."

"Here's what we know: she was an event planner, Gus found out she worked with an outfit called Events Unlimited that has an office downtown. It would explain how she was able to do so much traveling. Thirty-four years old, never been married. Lives with her parents, Letitia and Walter. Joan has apparently been following Evan all over the U.S.—well, the eastern U.S., anyway."

Jim let out a low whistle. "Celebrity obsession? I can't imagine having to deal with that."

"Let me do the talking at first. Gus and I agreed I'm there today because she met their daughter at the opening night of *Carousel* and asked me to stop and offer our sympathy. So that article in *The Morning Call* is helpful, since they may have read that Gus is performing with Evan at Pocono Playhouse."

"Isn't this a follow-up call for you?"

"Technically, I don't want it to be. It needs to be more informal. I think if it's a condolence call Mrs. Cromer might be more receptive. The poor lady could barely talk when I saw her Thursday morning."

"You and I must be on our way to lunch or something? Like I don't spend enough time staring at your mug when we're on duty?" Both men laughed.

110

"Let's say I'm helping you buy a birthday present for Carol."

"Nah, I'd ask her sister to help me with that."

"Well, for Jimmy, then. We're headed for Fairfax, there's a great bike shop there."

"Five-speed?"

Mal grinned as his partner. "You're serious, aren't you?"

"Well, kinda. He'd sure love one, and he does have a birthday in a couple of months."

"Let's see, he'll be eleven, right? And Kathy is eight." Mal glanced up ahead and pointed to Jim's left. "That's the house."

They pulled up in front of a newer house, a raised ranch with a two-car garage and a deck. The doorbell was answered by an attractive blond woman of around sixty. She appeared drained and sad, though she was wearing makeup and her hair was carefully brushed. *Making an effort*, Mal thought sympathetically.

"I remember you. Detective Mitchell, isn't it? You were one of the officers who let me know about Joan."

Mal took the hand she extended. "I am so sorry for your loss, Mrs. Cromer. I'm not here officially today. My wife, Augusta McKee, asked me to stop by and offer her sincere condolences. She met your daughter Monday night at the opening of *Carousel* at the Pocono Playhouse in Pennsylvania."

"Please come in, Detective Mitchell." Letitia Cromer glanced somewhat nervously at Jim.

"This is Jim Edmonds."

"Your partner?"

"Yes, but as I said, this is not an official call. Jim and I are birthday shopping for his son, and I wanted to stop and see you before we go out to Fairfax."

"Please sit down, gentlemen." Her hand trembled slightly as she gestured for them to find seats. "May I offer you something? Coffee?"

"No, ma'am. That's kind of you, but we're fine," Jim said. "So sorry about your daughter. What an awful shock."

Mrs. Cromer wiped away a tear. "It certainly was. I'm surprised we haven't heard anything from Evan, and I was stunned when I learned he'd been questioned as a suspect. Joan told me not long ago they were talking of marriage."

"Then I take it you've met him," Malcolm remarked.

"Well…no, not yet. He's been so busy. Touring, you know, and then performing at Lincoln Center." She sighed. "I'm afraid my daughter doesn't—didn't—confide in me as I'd like for her to, Detective Mitchell. She's a busy young woman who does a great deal of traveling. She has a very responsible position. I'm not really sure I quite understand what she does—did."

"Thank you. You know, I believe I would like that coffee, if it's not too much trouble," Malcolm said.

"No, I'd like to have some, too." Letitia nodded and went into the kitchen.

"What are you doing?" Jim hissed.

Malcolm raised a hand. "Just a little investigating," he whispered. "Give me a few minutes."

Mrs. Cromer brought in a small serving tray with a cup of coffee for each of them, and spoons, napkins, cream and sugar.

"Is that your daughter?" Malcolm indicated a framed photo of an attractive young woman on one wall. *Soft features framed by light hair, stylishly coiffed. Maybe a college graduation photo, or maybe taken since to be used in her profession. Something about her eyes doesn't fit. They appear almost expressionless.*

Letitia followed his gaze. "Yes, that's Joan. Actually, she had it taken fairly recently." Her voice became wistful. "She looks younger than thirty-four, doesn't she?"

"Yes, she does. I hope you don't mind my asking…was Joan your only child?" Malcolm stirred a half-teaspoon of sugar into his coffee.

"Yes, she was. Do you have children, Detective?"

"Two sons."

"Then you don't know about that mother-daughter dynamic. Joan and I were close when she was a child, but we didn't get along too well during her teen years. It's not uncommon." Mrs. Cromer sipped her coffee. "I'm sorry to say with Joan it didn't change much when she went to U.C. She continued to live at home and we eventually built a separate apartment for her downstairs. Since leaving college she's separated herself from us to a considerable extent, but we're grateful to have her still here, even though she doesn't spend much time with us."

"What was her course of study, may I ask?" Malcolm said.

"Her major was sociology. I'm not sure how she ended up working for that event planning organization—Events Unlimited. Joan worked with them for nearly ten years and was very successful."

Another sip of coffee. "She had a few friends in high school, and I'm sure she continued to enjoy friendships afterwards, but I seldom met anyone she spent time with once she graduated from Withrow. Joan didn't seem to want me in her life. Though I did meet a couple of the men she was involved with."

So they were estranged, thought Malcolm. *Despite being under the same roof.*

"Since she met Evan, she's been different. Excited. Happier than I've seen her in a long time" A ghost of a smile. "We had some nice conversations recently. As I said, she hinted that marriage might be in her future."

"One thing that might be helpful for the police in Pennsylvania to know, Mrs. Cromer, is whether Joan knew anyone else there. Maybe friends of Evan's? Or family?" Malcolm took a last swallow of his coffee.

"The police officer from Pennsylvania asked me the same question when he called. Trooper LaBar. No, Joan never mentioned anyone. I had forgotten all about this when I talked to him, but Joan did mention that Evan wanted her to meet his family while they were in Pennsylvania. They live nearby where she was staying, I believe. Well, no, I think she said someplace near Scranton. I've heard of Scranton."

"Do you suppose there might be something in her apartment that could be helpful to the Pennsylvania State Troopers who are investigating her case? Something that might mention someone else she knew or was expecting to meet while she was there? Maybe a letter?"

Mrs. Cromer stood. "I have a key to her apartment, Detective. We can go downstairs and you're welcome to look around."

They entered through a small combination sitting area-kitchenette. Letitia Cromer flipped on a light and Malcolm noted a small desk in the corner. When she opened the door to the bedroom and turned on that light, all three of them stared silently at the wall.

Carefully framed photos of Evan were arranged in groupings, with some framed newspaper clippings in the mix. Mal quickly counted at least twenty of them. Six photos were professional headshots of Evan. Several were clipped from newspapers, either of interviews or group shots with other cast members. At least three reviews from different newspapers and magazines. The headshots were artfully arranged in a circle at the center of the wall, all 8x10 photos in gold frames. The others were grouped around them with frames of different sizes and composition, some wood, some crafted from cardboard and fabric.

Around the entire display intertwined vines, dotted with occasional pink and white flowers, had been artfully painted. *Joan Cromer's world*, thought Malcolm. *She created a work of love here...but then she went much further*, he noted as he took in the rest of the wall, which was covered with childish scrawlings: "Joan & Evan forever," "Mrs. Evan Llewellyn," "Evan loves Joan," written with permanent markers. Malcolm glanced at Jim, whose mouth had dropped open.

Just one photo of Joan and Evan together, a small candid snapshot, sat beside her bed, a single artificial rose twined around it. It looked as if it had been snapped in a hotel bar or a lounge.

It struck Malcolm as indescribably sad, this display of a disturbed mind. *Did this obsession cost Joan her life?*

"Oh my…I never expected this." Mrs. Cromer dropped down on the bed abruptly. "I don't even know what to say."

Jim started to speak and Malcolm frowned, shaking his head slightly.

"It's hard to know exactly what this means, Mrs. Cromer. It's obvious she cared very much for Evan."

Letitia gazed up at him with tears in her eyes. "Yes, she did. We're…making arrangements to have her…remains brought back to Cincinnati as soon as possible."

"Hopefully that can happen before long," Jim said.

Malcolm put a hand under Mrs. Cromer's elbow and helped her to her feet.

"I wish I could be more helpful, Detective Mitchell," she said.

"I noticed a desk in the other room," Mal replied. "Do you think there might be something helpful in there?"

"Yes, there might." Letitia turned off the light as they exited the bedroom. She sank down on the small settee while Malcolm quickly looked through the desk.

"These letters from Evan might be a great help." He held up a stack of several pages, opened letters with no

116

envelopes. "May I have your permission to look through them and have copies made? I'll try to get them back to you this afternoon."

Mrs. Cromer, her head resting on one hand, waved the other. "Keep them, Detective. I don't want them."

Jim and Malcolm exchanged glances.

"It's no trouble. One of us will drop them off in the next couple of days," Mal remarked. "We can just leave them at the door, if you'd prefer."

"Yes, all right. That's fine."

"You've been extremely helpful, but I think we've overstayed our welcome, Mrs. Cromer." Jim said.

Mal extended a hand toward Letitia. "Here's my card. If you'd like to talk, please call me at any time."

Mrs. Cromer struggled to her feet. "I'm sorry, Detective. Obviously, there is a lot about my daughter I didn't know." She accepted the card. "Thank you. Yes, I'll be in touch."

"Thank you for the coffee, ma'am. Again, my heartfelt condolences for your loss."

Jim beat Malcolm to the car. Once inside where they couldn't be heard, he let it out. "Man, oh, man. Some bad vibes in that room, for sure."

Malcolm snorted with laughter. "*What*? 'Bad vibes?' Where'd you hear that?"

"Leo Underhill. The cool morning guy on WNOP, Radio Free Newport. You never listen to it, do you?"

"Define 'bad vibes.' And I turn it on once in a while, but it's too far out for an old guy like me."

"Weird. Strange. That wall in Joan's room."

"It was all of that. Joan was pathologically obsessed with Evan. I think what we just saw proved that. I need to talk to the people Joan worked with. She was part of that organization for nearly ten years and apparently did a good job for them. They may know something."

"You want to head down there now? They might be open, even though it's Saturday. Especially if there's an event going on locally."

"Yeah, I want to do that." He grinned. "I didn't tell Augusta, but I was able to get an early flight out tomorrow to Newark and I can be at her uncle's in time for lunch. She's not expecting me until Monday night. Can you take these letters and get photos of them for me?"

"You've got it. Anything else you need?"

Mal slapped the dashboard. "Wait! Stop the car."

Jim abruptly slowed and pulled to the curb. "What?"

"*Damn.* I should have called for a traffic cop to photograph that wall. It crossed my mind momentarily, but I was feeling sorry for Letitia Cromer. That's important evidence as well."

"Roger that," Jim agreed. "Want me to set that up and go back to the Cromers? I'll try to make it as painless as possible."

Malcolm sighed. "Yeah, we'd better do that. It's important for you to keep Mrs. Cromer on our side, though. Try not to alienate her. There may be more that comes up once I get to Pennsylvania that she can be helpful with."

Jim nodded. "I'll handle it. I think she likes me." He put the car in drive and pulled away from the curb.

"Here's what I have to do pronto," Malcolm said, frowning. "Let the Chief know what's happened as a result of my being involved in this. Especially what we learned today. I'll call Trooper LaBar ASAP so he knows I'm bringing possible evidence to him. Maybe we can meet on Monday."

Jim grinned. "Big city cop visiting the boonies. How do you think that's gonna fly?"

"I guess we'll find out. I don't want to step on anybody's toes, for sure, but I'm happy to help if I can."

"Yeah...but your wife is a friend of their prime suspect."

"I don't even know the guy. I'm just providing puzzle pieces for LaBar. Gus claims Evan Llewellyn is innocent. Well, if that's the case, then who murdered Joan Cromer? At the moment the only person the PSP is aware of even knowing her is Llewellyn."

"Maybe there's something in the letters."

"Doubtful. But these items are my ticket to connect with this case."

"Unofficially."

"Right. Unofficially." Both men laughed.

Chapter 9
Evan

Sunday, June 12
12:45 p.m.

Mal pulled up to Lenny's house in Buck Hill just before one, after an uneventful, pleasant drive from Newark Airport. Suitcase in hand, he ran up the steps and rapped on the front door.

Evan Llewellyn opened the door and his eyes widened as he became aware of exactly who stood facing him. He took a moment to size Malcolm up.

Mal realized he was doing exactly the same. *About 6'1", 185 lbs. Muscular. Medium brown hair, gray eyes. Damn, he's even better-looking in person than he is in his pictures.*

Evan broke the impasse, grinning wryly. "Detective Mitchell, I presume?" he asked in a conspiratorial voice.

Mal responded with an equally crooked grin and a nod.

Evan's grin broadened as he called toward the kitchen. "Augusta, there's someone here to see you."

"Who is it? Oh, never mind. Give me a minute," she replied from the kitchen, somewhat testily. Augusta disliked yelling.

The men exchanged amused glances as Mal stepped through the door and placed his suitcase on the floor.

Dish towel in hand, Augusta briskly walked in from the kitchen, but stopped short when she saw Malcolm. She gasped and flew into his arms. Mal kissed his wife warmly and she snuggled against him. "Oh, I am *so* glad to see you." She murmured against his neck. "I didn't expect you until Monday."

Mal noticed Evan heading toward the kitchen and silently thanked him. "I worked a little magic so I could surprise you." He caressed Augusta's face. "Your tear ducts are leaking."

"I know. I can't help it." She pressed her face against his. "I don't do as well without you, you know."

Augusta took a step away from Malcolm. "Oh, I need to introduce you...." She looked around. "Oh, dear. That was rude. I guess you and Evan introduced yourselves?"

Mal chuckled, "We figured out who we were when he answered the door." He pulled her back into his arms and kissed her again.

Augusta motioned to Mal's suitcase, keeping the other arm around his waist. "I'll show you to our room, Detective," she said softly. "The staff can hold lunch for a few minutes."

***

"I'm sure this is the last thing you'd like to hear, Evan," Malcolm said. "But both you and Garrett need to be aware I'm providing the Pennsylvania State Police with what could be additional evidence in this case."

Garrett took a final bite of his lunch. "As a courtesy of the Cincinnati Police Department."

"Yes. I can't go into specifics, but it confirms Joan Cromer was obsessed with Evan."

"Which means it could also implicate him in her death," Garrett commented.

Evan pushed his plate away, staring gloomily at his half-eaten lunch. Some of Milly's specialties: chicken salad, Greek salad, fresh fruit salad. Rolls from a local bakery.

"It doesn't surprise me." Elbows on the table, he leaned his head on his hands. "Len has several psychology books in his library, and I've been reading about erotomania. A pathological obsession with another person, generally a celebrity."

No one responded, and he continued, "Now I know how Susannah must have felt." He glanced around. "Augusta and I met when we performed together in an American opera, *Susannah,* which was loosely based on the story of Susanna and the Elders from the *Book of Daniel.*"

Augusta explained, "When Carlisle Floyd wrote his adaptation—during the McCarthy era—he set the story in Appalachia. He wanted to make a point about a lie taking on a life of its own when repeated loudly enough and for a long enough period of time."

Evan nodded. "In the opera, Susannah is bathing in what she thought was a secret place, and these young church Elders discover her and spy on her. To cover up their lecherous feelings, they accuse her of being a seductress. Nobody will believe she's innocent, especially the itinerant preacher I played, an absolute king of hypocrisy named Olin Blitch, who seduces the disheartened Susannah. When he realizes she was a virgin, he confesses his sin to the congregation of the church."

Augusta picked up the story from there. "Only they refuse to believe him about her innocence, and she is ostracized and forced to leave her home. The point being that even if you're telling the truth, just as witnesses did with Senator McCarthy, many people will choose to believe the often-repeated lie."

"In my case, I keep telling whoever will listen that I didn't kill Joan," Evan said. "But I'll be damned if I can find a way to prove it."

Silence ensued at the table for a moment, until Garrett spoke up. "You've got your whole team together, now, Evan. And your fans are behind you. Maybe we can't prove your innocence yet, but on the other hand, the prosecution can't prove you're guilty, either. I'm betting we find answers before they do."

Milly jumped up. "Peach cobbler for dessert. Len, come help me serve."

Evan took a long drink of water and relaxed slightly. "Well, I have some better news to share. My cousin Rhys is coming down from Carbondale to stay a few days to cheer me up. He's made a reservation at Skytop Lodge."

"Evan has told me about Rhys," Augusta said. "The cousin who was kind of Evan's champion when he was growing up."

"Yeah, he was. For a long time, Rhys was the only person in my family who supported my desire to sing. Eventually my mom got on board when my chorus teacher convinced her I had a shot at this." Evan leaned back in his chair. "Rhys and I were pretty close as kids, even though he's two years older. I think one reason he backed me up was because he loved to sing. And he was good. So, he could understand why I had such a strong desire to try. It'll be good to see him."

"I'm sure it will," Mal remarked. "Did he share your ambition? I mean was it something he considered at one time for himself?"

"Maybe. I honestly don't know. He's a brilliant guy who has two degrees in engineering. He worked in the pits for a time alongside his father. And then later, after Uncle Dave died." Evan glanced around the table. "Have you heard of the Knox Mine Disaster?"

Len fielded that question. "I may be the only one at this table who knows about it. Back in 1959, a subsidiary of the Knox Coal Mining Company was tunneling under the Susquehanna River to get to a particularly rich vein of coal."

"*Under* the river? That sounds dangerous," Milly remarked.

"Well, if they had taken the proper precautions, it could have worked out. But they neglected to do that, and as a result they actually broke through the ceiling of the shaft—which was the Susquehanna riverbed."

"Holy—" Garrett exclaimed. "And the Susquehanna flooded the mine. I can't even imagine what that was like."

"It *is* hard to imagine," Len said. "Millions of gallons of water pouring through an enormous whirlpool near the riverbank. It took an unprecedented effort to stop the flooding. They tried throwing everything imaginable into the river to plug the hole, including railroad boxcars. They finally had to divert the flow of the Susquehanna around an island in the river to actually see the enormity of the hole. It was filled with tons of clay and rock and a concrete cap covered the hole itself."

Len sat back. "It will probably prove to be the final blow to anthracite coal mining in the Wyoming Valley," he concluded.

"Most of the men who were working at the time survived," Evan told them. "Twelve did not. And their bodies were never found." He paused. "One of those men was my uncle, David Llewellyn. Rhys's father. Rhys was…he had a difficult time with his father's death. He ended up leaving home for a while. The better part of a year, in fact."

Len turned to Evan. "I thought you said you and your cousin grew up together in Carbondale. How was it your uncle died in the Knox Mine?"

"Well, in the early fifties the mines in Carbondale started to decline. Uncle Dave had a good offer from the Knox Mine, and he and my Aunt Ginny decided it wasn't too far from home. They had friends in Forty Fort, so they relocated in 1955." Evan shook his head. "How could they have known what an awful choice that was?"

"What does Rhys do now?" Milly asked. "You said he has two engineering degrees. Degrees in mining?"

"At the moment he's working on a project he's trying to sell to one of the companies in Carbondale which is still operating. That's actually hard for me to understand." He leaned forward, elbows on his knees. "After Uncle David was lost, I thought Rhys was done with everything about coal mining. The mines destroyed the land. And killed a lot of miners one way or another. Fires, floods, cave-ins, black lung disease." He gazed off into the distance. "As glad as I was to make another life for myself, it haunts me to think what I escaped. What could easily have been my fate."

Evan stood and gripped the back of his chair. "And now this. Being suspected of murdering a woman I spent one weekend with. Some kind of…retribution, maybe?"

"Oh, what utter nonsense, Evan." Milly stood and started clearing the table. "For that ridiculous remark you get to do KP with Len and Garrett. And while you're at it, get your head into *Carousel* and Billy Bigelow. I'm sure you'll have another sold out house tonight."

"And you two." Hands on hips, she glared sternly at Malcolm and Augusta. "You can go back to whatever you were doing that made us hold up lunch."

Mal laughed, enjoying the sight of Augusta blushing. "I'd like to take a walk and enjoy this clean mountain air for a bit. Then I could do with a nap before the performance tonight."

"Early morning flights will do that to you," Milly observed.

"Come walk with us, Milly," Malcolm invited. *A good opportunity to get her take on Evan.*

The three of them started off at a brisk pace.

"So, Detective, it must have been interesting to have the door opened for you by Augusta's old paramour," Milly said breathlessly.

Mal laughed heartily, slowing their walk as he realized how hard Milly was working to keep up with her considerably taller friends.

"Paramour? For heaven's sake, Milly," Augusta groused, staring at her. "Nobody on the planet uses that word these days."

Milly stopped, obviously happy to have a chance to catch her breath. "Okay, then. Old flame? Old beau?"

"Yeah, that was a bit awkward for a minute, to be sure," Mal said. "What's your take on the guy?"

"He didn't strangle Joan Cromer," Milly responded promptly. "Although he had plenty of provocation. We can keep walking, but please remember I have short legs."

Malcolm laughed again. "My mom used to smack the back of my head when I did that to her. She wasn't much taller than you are. Feel free to follow her example."

"Thanks, Mal. I'll do that." Milly set the pace as they resumed their walk.

"Here's my take on Evan—a somewhat self-centered man who has a hard time making friends. But all-in-all, a man with a good sense of who he is and what he wants in life. Deep down, he's generous and caring. And when I observe his behavior around women, he's unfailingly respectful and courteous. Kind of old-fashioned about it, in fact. Old school, some people would call it."

Milly stopped walking and gazed at Malcolm directly. "Never in a million years could I imagine Evan being angry enough at any female to kill her."

"Noted," Mal told her.

Later as he lay with Augusta gathered close in his arms, her head on his shoulder, he pursued the subject. "Do you agree with Milly? There's no way Evan could have killed Joan? Remember, you told me how angry he was with her Monday night."

She leaned up on one elbow and gazed into his eyes. "He was angry, yes. It was controlled anger, thought. He attempted to reason with her. I told you he only touched her to pull her hands away from him."

Augusta shuddered slightly and moved closer to Mal. "I saw what Joan Cromer's murderer did to her. I will never believe Evan could be capable of that kind of rage."

"It must have brought back a bad memory for you as well." He caressed her back. "You once had a killer's hands at your throat."

"Yes, I did. The hands of Linnea Murphy's killer. You saved my life." She shivered slightly.

Malcolm held her close. "I'm sorry you went through that."

"I am, too. I'll never be able to forget any of it—seeing Joan Cromer and realizing what you saved me from."

"In time, the image of Joan will fade. Try not to dwell on it."

They rested quietly for a moment, Malcolm kissing her face softly as he felt her relax.

Augusta sat up, again gazing earnestly into Mal's face.

"When you watch Evan onstage tonight, and see the tenderness he projects as Billy…and especially when you hear him sing with such intense emotion…I think you'll understand better why I'm convinced he's innocent."

She was pensive for a moment. "Evan has—I don't know how to explain it. You know how some people strike you as, well, insincere? Phony? You don't feel you can trust them? You sense maybe even a touch of evil?"

Malcolm nodded. "Yes. You feel intuitively there's a problem. Something isn't right."

"Evan is the exact opposite. He reminds me of you, in a way, though you're very different. But there's something in both of you—you're just *good*." She caressed his face. "With you, I sensed it from the moment I met you. It shines in your very being. With Evan, I hear it when he sings."

Augusta's eyes welled with tears as she gave Malcolm a tremulous smile.

"I believe you're both on the side of the angels."

Chapter 10
A Cop Is a Cop

Monday, June 13
9:00 a.m.

The Criminal Investigation Office located in the Pennsylvania State Police Barracks in Mt. Pocono appeared to Malcolm as orderly as a military command post. Trooper George LaBar—a broad-shouldered, pleasant guy, close-cropped light hair, probably late thirties, dressed in suit and tie—extended a hand.

"Good to meet you, Detective Mitchell." A firm grip.

"Malcolm, please, Trooper LaBar."

A warm smile. "And call me George."

He motioned Mal to follow. Once they were seated at LaBar's desk Malcolm handed him the folder with copies of the letters Mrs. Cromer had given him, and photos of the wall in Joan's apartment Jim had provided with the help of Cincinnati's traffic bureau photographer. Mal watched as George examined the items, waiting to see what the lead investigator's reaction would be.

131

George looked up, frowning slightly. "You said Mrs. Cromer had been unaware of her daughter's obsession with Evan Llewellyn. That's surprising. That wall is disturbing."

"My understanding was that their daughter became very private from the time she entered college. Even though she continued to live in the same house, her parents had built a separate apartment for her in the basement. While Mrs. Cromer had keys, it appeared she hadn't used them until Saturday."

"Have you read these letters?" George tapped the folder.

"Yes. Romantic declarations of undying love. Soap opera stuff. It seemed obvious to me Evan didn't write them."

"Tell me again why you went back to the Cromers'?"

"You've met my wife, Augusta McKee. She asked me to stop by and offer her condolences."

"Even though she had not formally met Joan Cromer."

"I'm sure she felt a connection and legitimately wanted me to pass along her sympathy." He leaned forward. "But I'll be honest, George. Augusta is something of an amateur sleuth. There is no doubt in my mind she thought I might learn something that would be helpful to you. And possibly to her friend Evan. Frankly, I was surprised when Mrs. Cromer told me about the apartment—let alone showed it to me. That's when the cop in me came out."

"Llewellyn is your wife's friend, but not yours?"

"He's not from Cincinnati. Augusta met him some ten years ago when they performed together in Chautauqua, New York. As I said, I met him for the first time yesterday. I saw him perform last night in *Carousel* and was impressed. Augusta is convinced he's innocent."

"He's been completely cooperative." George leaned back in his chair. "I have to say he seems like an all-right guy, even though at present the evidence points to him."

"He's very much aware of that." Malcolm shifted his position slightly. "Look, George. It's your puzzle and I'm happy just to bring you a couple of pieces and let you figure out where they fit. I'm sure your interest is in finding the truth. Just as mine would be, if this were my case."

Mal sat back and glanced around the room. "This is an impressive facility. You gentlemen run a tight ship. The Pennsylvania State Police has that reputation."

LaBar looked at him appreciatively. "Well, the Cincinnati Police Department certainly is highly regarded. I understand your chief may be in line for Hoover's job."

"It'll never happen. Stanley Schrotel won't leave Cincinnati. He's had a number of offers, Chicago among them. The Chief has spent his entire life in the city he loves."

"Well, I can relate," George chuckled. "My family has lived in Monroe County for many generations. No way would I want to leave."

Malcolm leaned toward George. "Do you mind my asking—I know about the letters you found in Joan's room and the appointment book. Since Garrett Stoddard, who is a friend, is Evan's attorney, I would think if you'd found anything else, you'd have let him know about it, right?"

"No, there wasn't anything else unusual." George hesitated. "One thing I looked for: people obsessed with someone, particularly a celebrity, will often try to find a way to take a trophy from the object of their desire. Any little item: maybe a cuff link, a pen, something similar. We didn't find any such objects. Evan said he hadn't noticed anything missing after that weekend he spent with Joan."

Malcolm lifted an eyebrow. "You're good, George. Killers sometimes do the same thing…take a trophy."

"Yes, we searched Llewellyn's car and his room at Buck Hill Inn, including his luggage. Nothing suspicious."

"Augusta mentioned a note found on the windshield of Evan's car."

George nodded. "What you'd expect. Just a plea for Evan to come to Joan's room at Skytop, and the room number. I told Counselor Stoddard about it."

And a sample of her handwriting, Mal thought. "Here's something I'm attempting to understand, why Evan Llewellyn's family was so dead set against the career he wanted to pursue. He's been highly successful. Any idea what that's about?"

LaBar rested his elbows on his chair arms and steepled his fingertips. "Not just his family. It's that entire culture."

"Coal mining is a culture?"

"Very much so. Do you know anything about underground anthracite coal mining?"

"Not really. It seems like a dangerous profession, though, from what I've heard about mine disasters. Fires, floods, cave-ins. And black lung disease, which sounds awful."

"It's all of that, and more. Black lung disease is a debilitating and usually fatal condition caused by inhaling coal dust over a long period of time. Miners are a close-knit community. Every day they go down into the pit, knowing there's a chance they might not make it out. They've formed a brotherhood. For the most part they look out for each other as all warriors tend to. They take great pride in what they do, and want to be the miner or the team that brings out the most coal during their shift. It's common for sons of miners to become miners."

"That makes sense. What about family life?"

"The family is important. Sons in particular. It can be difficult for a miner if his son chooses to follow another profession." He leaned back. "One more thing: a good miner can earn quite a bit of money—as long as his health holds up."

"Which explains some things about Evan Llewellyn. He's told us he had only one family member who supported his choice, a cousin. And, of course, attempting a career as a professional performer is a crap shoot. Hardly a sure thing."

"I would agree. But your wife why is she so sure Llewellyn is innocent? And you said she's kind of an amateur sleuth?"

Malcolm chuckled. "As a matter of fact, she's pretty good at it. I met her when I was working on the murder of a student at one of the colleges where Augusta teaches. She provided me the information I needed to apprehend the perp. As for her friend Evan—that's the other side of my lady. Music is her life, her passion. She can't believe a person who can sing as expressively as Llewellyn does could be capable of killing someone the way Joan Cromer was killed."

"He must be really something. Maybe I should try to catch a performance of *Carousel*," LaBar mused.

"I highly recommend it." Malcolm stood. "Thanks for educating me about coal miners. You know how to reach me, and if there is anything at all I can do to help, I'd be grateful for the opportunity. This is a fascinating case."

"Thank you, Malcolm." George stood and extended his hand. "I'll keep that in mind. Let's talk again if you come across any more puzzle pieces. In the meantime, I hope you're able to enjoy your stay in the Poconos."

"Oh, I definitely will. I want to climb Mt. Minsi and Mt. Tammany while I'm here."

"So, you know about our Delaware Water Gap," George laughed.

"Yes, I was here last fall for a short weekend. My wife and her uncle drove me through the Gap, and ever since I've wanted to come back and climb those hills. In fact, Augusta and I plan to climb Mt. Minsi this afternoon."

"Enjoy the views," George said. "They're pretty incredible."

***

In the dining room of Skytop Lodge, Augusta was receiving her own education about an aspect of underground mining. Evan had invited her to join him, Emily, and his cousin Rhys for a late breakfast while Malcolm visited the PSP Barracks.

Rhys greeted her warmly when Evan introduced them. "The fabulous Augusta McKee. I've heard a lot about you, all of it good. It's great to meet you." An attractive man, a definite family resemblance though Rhys had dark hair and eyes and wasn't quite as tall as Evan.

"If you don't mind, I think I'll have myself a Bloody Mary," Rhys continued. Emily and Augusta ordered mimosas, since there was no performance that night. Evan had grapefruit juice. They all opted for eggs Benedict and fresh fruit.

Their drinks were served, and the women listened to the cousins reminiscing about life as children and teenagers in Carbondale. Augusta was sure her eyebrows were lifted as much as Emily's when the two men joked about playing in and around abandoned mines as kids.

"I think we've shocked the ladies, Evan," Rhys quipped, waving his hand. "I guess it's hard to imagine unless you grew up in a mining community."

Evan laughed heartily. "I imagine so. Remember Big Plains Number One?" He turned to Emily. "We thought of that old mine as ours. That's where Rhys taught me to fight."

"Yeah, we had some good bouts in there, for sure. Remember when you landed your first knockout punch?" He joined Evan in laughter as Emily and Augusta exchanged glances.

Talk shifted from light to more substantive conversation as Rhys started on his second Bloody Mary. "Here's what I'm doing, Evan," he said enthusiastically. "I'm trying to convince one of the coal mining companies to resurrect the Conowingo Tunnel Project."

"How could that happen?" Evan asked. "It was taken off the table over ten years ago, wasn't it?"

Their server arrived with their breakfast orders as Rhys continued. "I think I've come up with a way to make it work. Think what it would mean for Carbondale: a resurgence of anthracite mining. There are still millions of tons of rich coal in that seam, just sitting there. And despite everything, this country still depends largely on coal for energy."

Augusta took a taste of her eggs Benedict. *Oh, so good.* Dabbing her lips with her napkin, she said, "Would you kindly enlighten Emily and me as to what on earth you're talking about?"

"Sure." Rhys picked up Augusta's water glass and held it up. "It's all about water. A drop of water always finds the lowest point, and the more mines that were dug, the more the streams and creeks drained into them." He replaced the glass with a flourish. "That meant the more the mines had to be pumped out. Before long, the cost of pumping began to outweigh the profit for removing coal. So, one solution—drain the mines." Rhys again picked up Augusta's glass, this time tipping his head back and gulping all the water from it. Augusta didn't join in the laughter.

Rhys signaled their server to bring Augusta another water glass as Emily commented, "You mean all the mines in this part of the state? That's a large area, right?"

Rhys chuckled. "Oh, it's an enormous project. It's considered 'audacious' and 'preposterous.' You're talking about a tunnel under the mines that would eventually be about two hundred miles long, ending up at the mouth of the Susquehanna River. Individual mines along the route could connect to the tunnel."

"One big problem," Evan remarked. "Dumping all that waste water into the Susquehanna and Chesapeake Bay. So, there was another thought, directing the tunnel to the Atlantic Ocean. Probably more of a challenge."

Rhys shrugged. "Well, the idea was discarded in 1954 as too costly in both time and money. But a serious five-year study by the Commonwealth of Pennsylvania along with the federal government proved it could be done." He leaned back, looking satisfied with himself. "The point is, I think I have a way to cut the cost in half, and the time down even more. How about that? I might be the savior of the anthracite coal industry in Northeastern Pennsylvania."

Plates were cleared and coffee poured while Rhys continued to pontificate after ordering his third Bloody Mary. Augusta observed him more closely. *Well, he seems very caught up in his project. But after what Evan said, I'm surprised. I thought Rhys hated everything about mining.*

Emily rolled her eyes at Augusta, indicating with a slight movement of her head she needed to escape to the ladies' room.

"Excuse us," Augusta said. Rising to her feet, she followed Emily from the dining area.

"My goodness, that man talks a lot, doesn't he?" Emily observed, adding a touch of lipstick as she glanced in a mirror. "I guess if I were a coal miner, I might find it fascinating."

"It does sound far-fetched." Augusta applied pressed powder lightly to her nose. "An underground tunnel from here all the way to the Atlantic Ocean? Resurrect the anthracite coal mining industry?"

In the mirror, Emily's eyes met Augusta's. "Well, my concern is, is it cousin Rhys or the alcohol talking? I have to tell you I was becoming extremely uncomfortable. I've witnessed that exact sort of behavior from my mother more than once."

Augusta knew from some backstage conversations with Emily what a difficult childhood she'd had. An alcoholic mother, an absentee father. A heroic older brother who tried to fill in for both parents. And as had happened with Evan, a high school music teacher who, upon hearing the promise in Emily's voice, had arranged for lessons with a teacher in her home town on a "scholarship"—which Emily later learned meant the high school teacher paid for her lessons.

"Mom would be full of enthusiasm about a new project," Emily continued. "A new apartment, a job interview she was sure would work out...but nothing ever came of them. Rhys is painting this picture of 'pie in the sky by-and-by,' and Evan sits there, hanging on his every word. Just as I used to with my mother's flights of fancy."

"I'm sure you know their history," Augusta responded, dropping her compact into her purse and facing Emily. "Rhys was the first person—and only person for a long time—who gave Evan any encouragement in his desire to sing. That meant the world to him."

Emily shook her head. "I don't know about Rhys. I don't think I trust him." She paused. "It strikes me that maybe he's decided it's time for payback from Evan. 'I supported your dream, now you need to support me by investing in my pie-in-the-sky project.' I wouldn't put it past Rhys to figure Evan owes him. I mean literally—financially."

Augusta lifted an eyebrow. "So young, yet so wise. I think you may be reading him correctly. This is a tricky situation, though. You don't want to alienate Evan. Try to play nice."

"I'll do my best," Emily said, frowning slightly. "But honestly, I wonder about leaving Evan alone with Rhys. It might be a good idea for one of us to be in the mix at all times."

Augusta had learned to appreciate Emily's intelligence and intuition when they had found time to discuss their characters' close relationship. And she was impressed with how protective Emily was being of Evan. *I can see a possible future for the two of them,* she smiled to herself.

As the two women headed back to their table, it suddenly struck Augusta how much Rhys and Evan resembled each other when seen from a distance. *Different coloring, but their features are very similar,* she mused. *Similar enough that if Rhys had been in the Playhouse parking lot last Wednesday night, someone glancing at him could easily mistake him for Evan...but Rhys didn't even know Joan, so how could he have a reason to kill her?*

Chapter 11
The Top of the Mountain

Monday, June 13
2:00 p.m.

"Do you recall what I said about how some people strike you the wrong way when you first meet them?"

Augusta and Mal were on their way to the Delaware Water Gap to climb to the top of Mt. Minsi, the cliff on the Pennsylvania side of the Gap. Mal had wanted to make this hike since their visit the preceding spring.

"Yes, I do," Malcolm replied. "That's how Rhys affected you?"

She turned toward him. "He's charming, but he works too hard at being charming. Emily commented on his behavior being similar to her mother's at times. Emily's mother had a drinking problem. Rhys downed three Bloody Marys during breakfast. He didn't seem impaired, though."

"Well, he probably wouldn't if he's an alcoholic." He glanced at her. "Why does this concern you, anyway?"

"It's not Rhys's behavior so much as the way Evan responds to him. There's still a little hero worship there, even though both men are in their forties."

Augusta shifted her gaze to the front window, pointing as she spoke. "You need to turn right just up ahead, past that old inn—The Deer Head. And then take the first left."

Soon they arrived at the parking lot next to a small lake, Lake Lenape.

"Looks like there are two ways up," Malcolm commented.

"We're using the Appalachian Trail for our hike," Augusta told him. "The views are much better and it's a good climb."

At the beginning it was a gradual ascent, clearly marked and evidently popular: they passed several family groups on the way up. Mal and Augusta enjoyed the view as they walked, Malcolm noting the variety of trees as they watched branches dancing in the wind.

"There isn't usually this much of a breeze along this part of the climb," Augusta said. "It's keeping the bugs in check today."

Mal chuckled. "We're both familiar with bugs where we live. Lots of birds to help control the bug population here."

Augusta started up a rocky section of the path and stumbled on the rough terrain. Malcolm caught her, saving her from a fall.

"I guess I should stop talking," she remarked, catching a breath and giving him a hug.

At their first stop there was a clear view of the Delaware River below. They could see Mt. Tammany, the mountain on the New Jersey side of the river, still above them but not far south of where they stood.

"Wow." Mal stood awe-struck as he gazed at the panorama before him.

"Tell me what you're thinking," Augusta said softly.

"It's kind of like…being lost in time. We're right here, standing close to this geological process that formed over millions of years."

Augusta remained quiet for a long moment before she spoke. "Yes, exactly. It is quite something, isn't it?"

Engrossed in the remarkable vista, Mal lifted the binoculars Len had insisted they bring. "Almost forgot about these." He adjusted them, then gazed down at the river. "I know I said it when we were here last fall, but the Delaware River is beautiful. So clean."

"We could rent a canoe before we leave if you want to experience it more closely."

"I'd like that." He grinned at her. "Think we could entice Garrett and Milly to join us for that kind of outing?" They laughed; both of their friends had declined their invitation for this afternoon's climb.

After that first stop the trail became steeper and much rockier, forcing them to concentrate on where they were stepping. Augusta had to stop for a moment. "I'd forgotten how strenuous this is," she panted. They continued their upward ascent and she stopped again, turning to Malcolm.

"Here's where we have the best view, even though we're still not quite at the summit." They stepped onto another rock outcropping, and directly across from where they stood, the impressive, rugged face of Mt. Tammany greeted them.

Mal stood enthralled. "I don't know if I've ever felt this at one with nature," he said softy. "This is why I knew I wanted to tackle these cliffs when we were here last fall." He continued to stare across at the mountain and the wilderness beyond which faded into a soft blue far in the distance.

"You know what it is? It's an affirmation." He lowered the binoculars and gazed at Augusta. "What I do can get so ugly. Knowing there's such beauty in this old world gives me hope. I'll never forget being here. Let's stay for a few more minutes." He took Augusta in his arms, gently wiping away a tear that trickled down her cheek.

They found rocks to lean against as they continued to collect memories in quiet companionship, passing the binoculars back and forth. Len had also provided canteens, and they gratefully drank from them before continuing the climb to the actual summit.

Once at the top, Mal looked to the far horizon to the south. "Is that the bridge where we crossed the Delaware last fall when we were here? I think the town is Portland?"

"Yes, Portland." She rested a hand on his shoulder. "Being up here makes you understand why people love mountains, doesn't it?"

"Yeah. It sure does. If I lived here, I'd make this hike often."

Augusta hugged him. "I believe you would."

They lingered a while longer before retracing their footsteps down the mountain.

On the drive back to Barrett Township Malcolm resumed their discussion about Rhys. "Lenny called some people he knows this morning at the Big Plains Mining Company. They've hired Rhys on a retainer to investigate a project."

"Rhys told us something about that at breakfast," Augusta confirmed. "He said he wants to resurrect a program which was originally studied several years ago by both the federal and the Pennsylvania governments."

"The Conowingo Tunnel Project. Len was informed the BPMC gave Rhys six months to prove he can make it happen." They drove through the tree-lined streets of Stroudsburg, a large borough and the seat of Monroe County. "This is nice."

"Stroudsburg has its own charm. And some excellent shops."

"Which you no doubt intend to visit," Mal chuckled. "Len doesn't know Rhys, but he once met his father. He described David as a miner through and through."

"Knowing that his father died in the Knox Mine disaster, it's surprising Rhys is making an attempt to resurrect the tunnel project."

Mal turned right onto North Ninth Street. "This is correct, isn't it? We want Route 611 North."

"Yes, this will take us to Mt. Pocono."

"Anyway, Len said he doubted anything could come of what Rhys is trying to do," Mal said.

"Emily commented about Rhys's plan sounding like 'pie in the sky.' It did seem a bit odd, considering what we were told about his reaction to his father's death."

Lenny met them at the door on their return. Mal grinned broadly and gave him a thumbs up. "It was everything you said it would be. I have to go back."

"Did Augusta break into song at some point? She actually did that the first time we climbed it when she was a kid."

Mal turned to Augusta. "You never told me you did that."

"You never asked," she replied with a grin. "Well, Lenny, I'm no longer a kid, though I did think for a moment about singing 'Climb Every Mountain' from the new Rodgers and Hammerstein show. I wasn't sure I could get through it without crying, to be honest."

"Maybe another role for you in the future, Augusta," Lenny laughed. "You'd make a great Mother Superior."

"We're getting ready to drive down to the Lehigh Valley for dinner," Milly told them. "Do you want to join us?"

"Do you mind if we pass?" Augusta asked. "I need a shower and a chance to put my feet up. I haven't done any climbing in a long time."

"No, not at all," Milly replied. "I told everyone I figured you two might appreciate a chance to catch your breath…some alone time."

Len and Evan took his car and headed for Skytop to pick up Rhys and then swing by the cast house for Emily, while Garrett and Milly followed in a second vehicle.

Augusta and Mal took advantage of the empty house, first taking a long, leisurely shower. Afterward, they napped for over an hour, raiding the refrigerator after they were up and dressed.

"Looks like Mil made food for us," Malcolm grinned. "Isn't this spinach pie? Just needs to be warmed up."

Augusta poured them each a glass of pinot grigio. "More Greek salad. And everything we need for kabobs. The woman is a food mill."

They carried their feast out onto the back porch and relaxed, enjoying the fragrant breeze wafting through evergreen trees, accompanied by the sound of bird songs.

"Almost like home, except there are more trees and Fritz is missing," Augusta said.

Malcolm grinned. "By that I take it you mean you miss Fritz?"

"Of course, I do. And wouldn't he love it here? But I'm sure he's having a great time with Caruso."

"I'll call Trevor in the morning to see how everything is going. They were kind to take him Saturday afternoon so I could get up here sooner." He gazed at her, smiling. "Remember what we were doing last summer at about this time?"

"Oh, I certainly do." Augusta gripped her fork and pointed at Mal with it. "We were trying to find out who had killed two members of a string quartet. And we'd just returned from our honeymoon in Europe."

"Where I met an old friend of yours," Mal teased.

"Oh, I remember that well. You invited this French *inspecteur* to have drinks with us and deliberately never told me his name. When Jean-Luc walked into the hotel bar I almost fell off my chair." Augusta tilted her head and laughed.

"Another old boyfriend." They chuckled as they recalled the moment. Mal grew pensive. "I hope you never regret it, Augusta. Joining your life to mine."

"You know I won't. Why would you even say that?"

"I have this sense you could have married Evan. Don't tell me he didn't ask you."

"Well, yes, he did." Augusta lifted her glass of wine and watched the glow of sunset through the pale amber liquid. "I couldn't see myself in a long-term relationship with him. He had his life, I had mine. He was off to an extended tour of Europe, which eventually brought him international recognition. I had just bought my house. I loved—and still do—that I was teaching. You know that's who I am. Why would I give that up?"

She took a sip of wine. "Evan and I were an interlude."

Mal leaned close and rested a hand on the back of her neck. "What are you and I?"

She smiled. "A symphony. An opera. One that will never end."

"We're good together." He moved his hand to caress her face, gazing into her eyes.

"We are." She took his hand and kissed it. "I knew we would be. The time we spent together while you were working on Linnea Murphy's case showed me exactly who you are. I knew fairly early on that you were the one."

He smiled. "When I saw you again, all those years after I'd first seen you performing at the Summer Opera, I thought I might have been given a second chance. Those don't come along very often."

"No, they don't. And I remembered you—the young man with the intense blue eyes who asked for my autograph."

Mal laughed softly. "Oh, yes. And now here you are, my bride of one year. The love of my life…and even my co-detective at times. Working with me on yet another case, though I'm not sure I'm actually doing much with this one yet."

The sky had grown dark as they talked, and a sliver of a moon shone among the stars.

Augusta sipped her wine thoughtfully. "Mal, Emily and I made the obligatory trip to the ladies' room while we were at Skytop this morning. That's when she told me her concerns about Rhys."

"Len's driving him to the Lehigh Valley. They'll be in the car together for over two hours. Lenny will learn more."

Augusta waved a hand. "I'm sure he will. But here's something else—when we went back into the dining room, I was struck by how much Rhys and Evan resemble each other."

"Well, they are cousins."

"Yes, but it's more than that." She frowned. "I think if Rhys had been in the Pocono Playhouse parking lot on Wednesday night, he might easily have been mistaken for Evan."

Intrigued, Mal leaned forward. "That strong a resemblance, is it?"

"Yes, I believe it is. But what possible reason could Rhys have to murder Joan? So far as we know, he never even met her."

"And that's key to this case." Mal stood and walked to the railing, turning to face Augusta as he theorized. "You're convinced Evan didn't murder Joan. Let's accept that. Who could have killed her? It was someone who knew her well. That's the only explanation for the brutal way she was strangled."

"Which would rule out a robbery."

"Money was found in her purse—over four hundred dollars," Mal remarked.

"Joan was obsessed with Evan. Is it possible there was another man she was subjecting to the same treatment? Who might have seen her in the parking lot, accosted her, and killed her?"

"Not likely," Mal replied. "Joan was fixated on Evan. From what I understand about that kind of obsession, it's unlikely she would give another man any kind of attention. Also, her death took place at an odd time. The show started at 8:15, correct? Maybe 8:20 if the curtain had been held for late-comers."

Augusta nodded. "We've been told the coroner put the time of death at between 8:00 and 10:00. The couple who arrived late and identified Evan claimed they saw a man and woman in a heated argument at about 8:45."

"And I wonder about that as well." Mal returned to his chair. "Why was Joan in the parking lot near Evan's car at that time?"

"You know about the note Trooper LaBar found on Evan's windshield."

"Yes, she must have gone to his car deliberately to put it there so he'd see it when he left the theater after the show." He stood again and began to pace. "But how did she know where he parked?"

"Evan said she tried to speak with him after the performance Tuesday night. He told me he likes to get to the theater early and had probably parked in the same place both nights. Or all three nights, starting with Monday."

"Joan approached him during the after party on Monday, correct?" Mal said, stopping to gaze at Augusta.

"Yes, but that doesn't mean she wasn't aware of where he parked." Augusta paused. "He was staying at Buck Hill Inn. She was staying at Skytop."

Mal resumed pacing. "You're suggesting that on Monday or at least on Tuesday…she could have driven to Buck Hill, waited for him to get in his car and drive off, and then followed him to the Playhouse. Were there other actors arriving at about the same time?" He resumed his seat.

"There were. Several of them," she replied. "So, if that happened, chances are he wouldn't have noticed her. And then she could have done the same thing on Wednesday. She wouldn't have expected to see him until after the show ended, so she was taken by surprise on Wednesday night."

Augusta stared at Mal. "And there's this," she continued. "There was absolutely no reason Evan would have left the theater and gone out to the parking lot during the time he wasn't on stage that night. That makes no sense, especially with what you're suggesting, that he didn't realize she'd followed him."

Mal poured himself a second glass of wine. "I have to believe that whoever killed Joan was someone who knew her. She was murdered by someone who was enraged."

They heard the sound of cars pulling up outside the house, prompting them to take their empty plates and glasses into the kitchen. As they cleaned up, they heard Evan excusing himself and climbing the stairs.

Len, Garrett, and Milly were seated in the living room, obviously waiting for Augusta and Malcolm to join them.

"So, how was your dinner?" Mal asked.

"Excellent," Milly replied. "It's a great restaurant." She pointed overhead, put a finger to her lips and added in a low voice, "Rhys talked a lot. Some of it didn't make much sense."

"A genuine blowhard," Len added, keeping his voice low. "Drinks too much. Full of himself. I think

Evan began to grow a little weary of cousin Rhys's obvious desire for the limelight."

Garrett said, "This struck me as odd: as the three of us were walking out to the cars Milly and I were telling Rhys what a terrific city Cincinnati is, and Rhys agreed, saying that he was there last fall at a conference. Earlier we'd had the impression he'd never been there."

Milly added, "Augusta, I know you said Joan Cromer was an event planner in Cincinnati."

"Yes, she was," Augusta murmured.

"So, then I asked him casually where the conference was held and he said at the Netherland Hilton. Could that be important?"

"It's possible," Malcolm replied, slowly turning to glance at Augusta, who was already staring back at him. "The Netherland Hilton houses the offices of Joan's company, Events Unlimited. Joan and Rhys may actually have met each other there."

Chapter 12
The Burning Earth

Tuesday, June 14
10:00 am.

"How was it first discovered?"

"Some people who lived in one section of the west side of Carbondale began to notice things that weren't right," Len replied. "Banks of a creek that were warm in the dead of winter. Hot, in fact—ice and snow would melt quickly. Steam rising from the ground. The odor of burning sulfur."

"Good God, sounds like the entryway to hell." Mal shook his head. "And it's so pretty here."

"We're not in Carbondale yet. I took the long way around to show you more of the area, the part we call the Wyoming Valley. Carbondale is further north and east, so we'll backtrack a bit." Len signaled and passed the car ahead.

"Pennsylvania is a beautiful state," Mal observed. "Why is this area called the Wyoming Valley, anyway? I get the valley part, but the river is the Susquehanna."

"Wyoming is from an Indian word meaning 'big river flat.' It was inhabited by several native tribes, mostly part of the Iroquois Confederacy. You know, no matter how far I travel and how much I see, it's always a thrill to come back home. I need to help make good things happen here. I really love this place."

"I can see that," Mal chuckled.

"Anyway, back to the underground fire," Len said. "Those signs started to show up back in 1943. For the next two decades, it just got worse and worse. The fire continued to burn, directly under some of the houses. The residents couldn't walk across basement floors without boots because of the heat. Fissures began to open in their yards, their driveways…even in some of the streets. Houses tilted. Sinkholes opened all over the place."

Mal stared at Lenny. "Incredible. What did they do to try to extinguish the fire?"

"Everything. Trying to flush it out with water just made things worse. Engineers came in to study it and determined the size of the fire. They found it was burning as much as a hundred feet down and spread over at least a hundred and twenty acres with an unending source of fuel."

"And you're telling me people began to lose their homes?"

"Houses started falling apart. Pipes broke, floors shifted. Wallpaper peeled off walls from the heat.

Eventually one house and then another would be condemned. Oh, the company bought the houses, but didn't pay enough for the family to find one as nice as the one they had to leave. Some of those had been homes to a family for several generations. You have to understand, Mal, miners are proud people. Much of the time, the mining company actually holds the mortgage and the miners work years to pay it off. Their home is the only thing of value they ever have."

"And this was where the Llewellyn cousins grew up." A shake of his head. "No wonder Evan feels he escaped."

Len turned right onto a street lined with a mixture of homes and commercial establishments. "About ten years ago, the fire turned deadly. A couple was found in their home dead of carbon monoxide poisoning. "

"They wouldn't even have known they were breathing it in," Mal frowned, shifting in his seat.

"Right. In order to protect the west siders, gas inspectors were brought in. They checked every house still occupied twice every twenty-four hours. Homeowners left their doors unlocked so the inspectors always had access."

"Unbelievable. How did the residents feel about that?"

"They were fine with it. Lives were saved, some just in the nick of time. But so far as we know, no one else died as a direct result of carbon monoxide poisoning."

As they drove on, more houses lined the streets— mostly frame but some stone. Churches stood on corners, reminding Mal of parts of Cincinnati. "Where are we now? This is nice."

"This is the east side of Carbondale. It hasn't been affected by the fire, and hopefully won't be in the future. The effort underway to dig up the fire is more than impressive. But what you see here is very much what the west side of Carbondale used to be. And parts of it still are."

They drove across a viaduct and approached an area where steam rose in spots. No buildings anywhere, men guarding the site. Massive mounds of earth, some steaming and smoking, ringed the rim. Len parked the car, and as they opened the doors the acrid odor of sulfur permeated the air.

They walked closer to the pit, Mal finding it difficult to process the scene before him. The vast hole stretched across a wide area, the equivalent of many city blocks, its depth accentuated by the large piece of earth-moving equipment which appeared small at the bottom of the pit. More huge machines closer to the rim. Mal let out a low whistle and then stared, silenced by the enormity of devastation and destruction.

Len finally said, "It's not easy to believe this is real. Yet here it is. They're digging the entire area down to bedrock."

"What are their plans? Refill this…chasm…and then what?"

"There's talk of making it residential. But it wouldn't surprise me if it becomes commercial. That's still to be determined."

The men returned to Len's car. Mal, lost in thought, sat quietly as they drove away.

"We're meeting an old friend for lunch," Len told him. "Jack Davies. He knew David Llewellyn well, and has been close to Rhys for most of his life. He worked as a supervisor for the Big Plains Mining Company for many years."

"Don't introduce me as a detective. Let's keep this low key."

"Agreed. Your wife's an old friend of Evan's, and you're here to see the show and spend some time in the Poconos. Evan's in trouble, and Rhys has come to the Poconos to spend time with his cousin. We can let Jack take it from there."

Jack Davies, a pleasant, jovial man in his late sixties, needed no prompting to talk about his friend Dave Llewellyn and Dave's boy. "Rhys was always a super smart lad. Very protective of his younger cousin. He taught Evan how to fight, and many's the time the two of them took on three or more boys for giving Evan a hard time." He laughed. "Those two were quite a pair."

"Evan seems to still idolize his cousin," Len remarked.

"Ah, as well he should. Rhys did a lot back in the day to see that Evan had the chances he never got—to develop his talent."

"So Rhys was also a gifted singer?" Mal asked.

"That he was. But for Dave's putting his foot down and refusing to allow him to pursue music, Rhys could possibly be where Evan is today. Don't get me wrong."

Jack leaned toward Mal. "I don't think Rhys is a bit jealous of his cousin. He's proud of Evan."

Jack finished his first beer and the server immediately put a second in front of him as he gave her an approving smile. "Mind, I haven't seen Rhys for a few months. My feeling is his father's death changed him, as did his mother dying suddenly only about three months ago. I haven't seen him since the funeral."

"Sorry to hear that. I wasn't aware of it," Mal said.

Continuing to fish for information, Len remarked, "We were told Rhys left home for a time following the Knox disaster."

"That he did. Went to West Virginia and worked in a mine down there for several months. Then he headed out west and did the same in a silver mine. When he came back, he wanted to find a way to resurrect the Conowingo Tunnel Project. To revitalize anthracite mining in our valley."

"Yes, he seems to be on a bit of a crusade," Len agreed. "You said his father's death changed Rhys. In what way?"

Jack stared thoughtfully into his beer, seeming to weigh his words. "Sad to say, he did start drinking. Far too much. And he shut himself off from people. He'd become angry for little or no reason. Ginny—Rhys's mother—wanted to move back to Carbondale after the mine disaster, so I helped her with that. Rhys was around at the time, but he didn't give her much support. I mean he didn't think she should move back here."

"He thought she should have stayed in Forty Fort?" Len asked. "That would just be a reminder of her husband's terrible choice to relocate."

"I think Rhys didn't want to be in Carbondale. Or in Forty Fort. After the Conowingo project shut down he became depressed. He didn't have a steady job for nearly a year, just did odd jobs and worked part time for an auto body shop. Rhys wasn't happy when Dave decided to take the job with the Knox company, but Ginny insisted he move with them. You already know what happened after Dave's death."

Another swig of beer. "When Rhys left it really was kind of a relief to have him out of the picture for a time. He stayed in touch with his mother, though. Ginny has a lot of friends here, she did okay. Then while Rhys was out west. he started calling her more often, telling her he knew exactly what he wanted to do. After he got back, he let her know about his determination to make the tunnel project work. He hung onto that after she died, when the BPMC finally gave him a chance to prove himself."

"Do you think that could happen—the project could be revived?" Mal asked.

"Mr. Mitchell, a whole panel of brilliant people, some from right here in Pennsylvania and some with the federal government, spent nearly ten years trying to find a way to get that project off the ground. It never happened. Do I think one—well, let's call him a visionary—could do what they could not? No way in hell."

***

Augusta waited by the phone, her fingers on the handset as she made notes on a pad about what she planned to say. She lifted the handset to her ear and dialed.

"Events Unlimited. This is Brenda."

"Hi, Brenda," Augusta said, hoping she sounded perky and youthful. "This is Iris Mitchell from the Valley Anthracite Mining Company in Carbondale, Pennsylvania."

"Hi, Iris. What can I do for you?"

"Well, I'm a free-lance auditor and I'm going through the books for the past year. I found an item the company needs confirmation on, a conference attended by a Mr. Rhys Llewellyn. The thing is, we just can't find any information at all, and decided it must have been misplaced. Mr. Llewellyn is no longer with the company and isn't available for us to ask him about it, so it would certainly be a huge help if you can answer some questions."

"I'll certainly try. What can you tell me about the conference?"

"We know it was held in Cincinnati sometime during the past year, and it must have been for people involved with mining…maybe engineers? I wish I could tell you more, but right now that's pretty much all I have."

"Let me take a look. Can you hold, or would you like me to call you back?"

"Oh, I'm happy to hold. Thank you so much." *Don't gush, Iris. Well, I really am Iris Mitchell. Augusta Iris McKee Mitchell. It says so on my marriage certificate.*

Brenda returned after a few minutes. "I found him. We hosted a conference right here in Cincinnati in October of 1965 at the Netherland Hilton, 'The Future of Underground Mining.' Mr. Llewellyn attended as a free agent and stayed at the hotel. Maybe that's why the company records don't show anything, he or a sponsor could have covered his expenses."

"Oh, that would explain it. Can you give me the details?"

Brenda obliged her by providing particulars—dates, times, what Rhys had spent.

Now this is awful, but I have to do it. Augusta steeled herself. "You know, I met someone who works in your organization not long ago. Is there a chance she worked on that conference? I'd love to say hi if she's there—Joan Cromer?"

"As a matter of fact, Joan ran that conference." Silence for a long moment. "I'm so sorry to have to tell you this, Iris." Brenda's voice quivered and she paused again. "Joan was an important part of our organization for ten years. She died only a few days ago."

"Oh, no! How awful! Oh, I am so, so, sorry. Had she been ill?" *Augusta McKee, you are a terrible person.*

"No, it was very sudden. In fact, she died in Pennsylvania while she was visiting there."

"That's terribly sad, Brenda. My condolences to you and your co-workers. I wish I could say something helpful." *Should I ask her who Joan was visiting? No, don't push it, Augusta. Hang up the damn phone.* "Thank you again for your assistance," she said in a gentle voice.

Augusta replaced the phone receiver and walked to the window, staring out at the trees. *Joan had friends who cared; Brenda is grief-stricken. Joan's parents have lost their only child. Damn you, Rhys. I know you did it. But why?*

***

Evan pulled Mal and Augusta aside after an early supper at Len's, provided courtesy of Milly and Garrett. They planned to leave before seven to get to the theater.

"Are we picking Rhys up?" Augusta asked Evan.

He shook his head no. "I asked him to meet us there. I also told him I didn't want to go out after the show tonight."

Augusta and Malcolm exchanged glances.

"What's going on, Evan?" Augusta asked.

He ran a hand through his hair. "Something's not right. He's not the cousin I remember. The way he acted at dinner last night was…well, bizarre." He glanced from Augusta to Malcolm. "I'm concerned about him."

"Didn't you guys play golf this morning at Skytop?" Augusta asked. "Garrett joined you, I believe."

"Yes, and we picked up a fourth, another guest at the Lodge." He took a deep breath. "This isn't easy to talk about. I think Rhys cheated. The golfer who joined us as our fourth didn't say anything, but I think he was just being polite." He took another deep breath.

166

"I couldn't believe Rhys would do that. Could it be the alcohol? I'm sure you've both noticed how much he drinks." Evan looked from one of them to the other. "I don't understand what's going on with him. Out of the blue he made a remark about my Uncle Dave. 'I just want my father to be proud of me for once, that's why I have to make the tunnel project work.' He said that after our golf game. Maybe I'm reading this all wrong, but it seemed like a strange comment for him to make."

"When was the last time you saw Rhys?" Mal asked.

"At Christmas. I went home to visit my family. My Aunt Ginny was living in Carbondale again, and Rhys was there. He seemed okay then. A little distracted, but we had a good time together. He certainly wasn't drinking so much then. You know my aunt died not long ago?"

"I heard that today," Mal said.

"That's another thing. Rhys still talks about her sometimes as though she's still alive. It's as if he has to remind himself she's not here anymore."

"Len drove me to Carbondale today," Mal said, "and I saw what's happening with the fire. I'd like to get Rhys's take on this, he's a mining engineer. Draw him out. It could be he's just feeling a little out of his element being around show biz types."

"Maybe, but I doubt it."

When they arrived at the theater, Augusta turned to Mal. "I'll walk back with you," she said as they dropped Evan at the entrance and watched him go inside.

"Maybe we should open up to Evan about what you and I discussed," Augusta said. "We know Rhys attended

167

a conference Joan was in charge of in October. It's likely they met. We have no idea what might have transpired between them, but we need to find out."

"I'll get in touch with Jim tomorrow and ask him to go back to the Cromers'. He may find some answers, and we'll wait to see what he learns. But I agree, the fact that they probably met at that conference is a piece of the puzzle. But what might that meeting have led to? At the moment, there's no way to tell where that piece fits."

Mal pulled into a parking spot and leveled his blue eyes at Augusta. "I'm beginning to feel Rhys Llewellyn is a deeply troubled man, Gus. Rhys does drink a lot. Who knows how much longer he'll be able to keep it under control? Some of that could be from low self-esteem—mixed with a propensity for alcohol addiction. It's hard to tell for sure, but it makes me wonder if his father also drank to excess. A lot of miners do, I believe."

He pulled the keys from the ignition and opened his door. "After what I learned today, I can understand why. It's a tough life."

Augusta rested a hand on Mal's arm. "A lot of people lead difficult lives, Mal. You among them, but you don't abuse alcohol."

"Still, it happens, and it can happen to anybody given the right circumstances. More and more people agree with the experts who believe alcoholism is a disease; there's a good argument for that. And there's this: Rhys's alcohol addiction may mask a more serious mental health problem."

They sat quietly for a moment and Mal said, "When did Joan and Evan spend that weekend in Indianapolis?"

"About a year ago, sometime in late June of 1965. And then she followed him to Rochester only a few weeks later, and turned up again in Atlanta, I think in September." Augusta frowned. "So, if Rhys met Joan in October, which we feel fairly sure happened, by then she was completely obsessed with Evan."

Mal nodded. "I'll keep Rhys talking before the show and during intermission," He walked around the car and opened the door for his wife. "He may let something slip again, just as he did at dinner last night. In the meantime, don't you even think about it. Just escape into that whaling village in New England for the next couple of hours, Nettie Fowler."

Augusta kissed him and linked her arm through his. "Sounds like a plan. Have I told you recently how much I love you, Detective Mitchell?"

"You can say it as often as you like, Mrs. Mitchell," Mal grinned. "I never tire of hearing it."

Chapter 13
The Coal Miner's Son

"Let's not wake anyone up," Augusta whispered to Mal and Evan as they arrived back at Len's, but they opened the door to the sound of recorded music accompanying a lively conversation in the kitchen.

Milly stuck her head through the kitchen door. "Come on in, we're having snacks and beverages," she informed them.

"Apparently," Mal chortled.

Len appeared, plate and glass in hand. "Let's move into the library. It's too crowded in the kitchen."

"We have beer, wine, coffee, and iced tea," Milly informed them. Before long they were all settled comfortably in the library, enjoying Milly's delectable snacks and their choice of drink. Augusta noted Malcolm had opted for coffee instead of his usual beer, which meant he was staying in detective mode in hopes of learning more from Evan.

"I recognize that voice," Augusta said. "This is your new album, isn't it, Evan?"

"It is. I didn't realize Lenny had it." He held up a hand. "No arias. Musical theater, some of my favorite pop songs, and a couple of folk tunes." Evan took a long swig of beer. "Boring title, 'Evan Llewellyn Sings,' and it'll never be at the top of the charts. But it sure was fun to record."

Evan drained his beer and went into the kitchen for another. *Excellent, he's relaxing. He's very comfortable with us,* Augusta thought, her eyes meeting Mal's as she turned to him.

The next selection was a favorite of Augusta's, "This Nearly Was Mine" from *South Pacific*. She believed Richard Rodgers' waltzes were his very best compositions, and this was a heart-wrenching song of regret from the French planter Emile de Becque, who believes he has lost forever the woman he loves. *The role Evan was performing when Joan Cromer became obsessed with him,* Augusta thought.

Evan sang the piece with aching poignancy, using just the right vocal colors and musical nuance. *The love he's convinced he'll never recover.* Augusta glanced at Evan and his eyes met hers.

"Come to Europe with me, Augusta. Can you imagine how great that would be?"

"Evan, I'm complimented, but this is your adventure. Enjoy it to the fullest." Unspoken was my thought, *I have a happy and fulfilling life in Cincinnati. I love what I do and where I am.*

Augusta glanced away, aware that Malcolm, seated next to her, was watching.

The song ended on a sustained high note, sung with power and beauty. Enthusiastic applause from the listeners. "*South Pacific* next summer, Evan," Len said, to murmurs of agreement.

The introduction to the next song drew comments: it was Merle Travis's "Sixteen Tons."

"Trying to outdo Tennessee Ernie?" Garrett asked to general laughter.

"Why would you include this?" Milly asked.

"Why not? It's my heritage, folks." Evan proceeded to sing with himself for the rest of the number, his rich voice filling the room with the description of a typical miner's life: working long, back-breaking hours simply to stay alive and pay off his debts to the coal mining company, which basically owned him.

More applause followed and Evan stood and took a bow. "If it hadn't been for my mom, my high school chorus teacher, and my cousin Rhys, that would have been my life. But I sang this song for my daddy. He'll like it."

Mal leaned back and glanced at Evan. "I learned today Rhys had quite a voice himself."

"It's true, he did. Only thing…" Evan stared into his beer bottle. "I'm not sure Rhys had the genuine desire to do the work. I mean to study music seriously in order to do what I'm doing. Most people have no idea the amount of discipline required to learn to sing well."

He waved a hand. "Of course, Augusta and Milly do, and I guess you gentlemen probably do since you're in their lives." He shook his head. "That didn't come out right, did it? One more beer should do it." Evan stood and went into the kitchen. "Anybody else want one?" He called out.

"No, we're good," Garrett responded.

Len turned off the recording. "I'm headed for bed, troops. See you at breakfast."

Garrett started to stand and Mal said quietly, "Stay. We may learn something."

Evan returned and glanced around the room. "About my cousin Rhys." There was quiet. "I said something to Mal and Augusta earlier. Something isn't right with him."

"Why do you say that, Evan?" Mal asked. "We had a good time talking before the show and during intermission. He told me quite a bit about life in Carbondale and about your family. I didn't realize your fathers were twins."

"Yes, they were." A pause. "Did he talk to you about the Conowingo Tunnel project?"

"Actually, he didn't say much about that. I was surprised, because I'd heard he's been quite enthusiastic about what he sees as a great opportunity to bring anthracite coal mining back to life."

Evan leaned back in his chair again, one hand behind his head. "Yes, he's been talking about it a lot. He mentioned it briefly this morning. But mainly he asked me questions about Joan Cromer."

Augusta remarked, "Didn't you tell him about her when he first got here?"

"Yes, I told him what had happened recently. And last Christmas I talked to him about how she'd been pursuing me." He ran a hand across the back of his neck. "But it was more than that. Augusta, you remember how he was at brunch on Monday? Talking a mile a minute, full of big plans. And today he was…just the opposite. Subdued. Even a little belligerent. I never saw Rhys act that way before."

"What did he want to know about Joan?" Mal asked casually.

"Mainly, how she died. I told him all I knew was what I saw when I identified her body. He wanted details and I said I wasn't comfortable talking about it. I had a hard time understanding how anybody could…well, could brutalize a woman that way."

Augusta shivered involuntarily. "I don't believe I'll ever forget seeing her like that."

Evan leaned toward her. "I'm sorry, Augusta. I didn't think before I asked if you could come with me to the parking lot that night."

"No, Evan, it's fine, really. I'm grateful I was with you."

He grew quiet. "There's this," he said, staring at Mal. "Rhys asked me specifically about her hair. Her blond hair. Did the paper say that she was blond?"

"I don't recall," Augusta said quickly. She faked a yawn, covering her mouth with the back of her hand. "Well, I think we're all tired, and I for one need sleep."

They stood and returned dishes to the kitchen, where Milly and Garrett did KP duty. His face a study in confusion, Evan pulled Augusta and Malcolm aside.

"How did he know about her hair? Could Rhys have possibly met Joan? I don't understand how. She was dead before he got here."

"You said you talked about her when you were with Rhys at Christmas, and again when he first arrived. It's likely you mentioned that she had blond hair. I wouldn't worry about it." Mal soothed.

Once in their room, Augusta turned to Mal. "He knows."

"He might. Well, I'm calling Jim Edmonds first thing in the morning. But what Evan just told us could be another puzzle piece."

***

Wednesday, June 15
7:30 a.m.

"Three things," Mal said to Jim. "First, do some fishing and use Rhys's name to see if Mrs. Cromer reacts to that. Second, look around her room again. Now that I've given you all the information I have on Rhys, you may find something that connects the two of them. Third, ask if Joan ever showed her mother, or even discussed, any kind of 'trophy' item—most likely a piece of jewelry. Probably not a ring, but maybe a bracelet or a necklace. Ask if she ever saw something like that, and get a description if she confirms it."

"I'm on it, partner. I'll head over there as soon as I report to the Chief and let him know what's happening. When do you see LaBar again?"

176

"We left that open ended, but if you find anything, I believe I'll need to get in touch with him. Of course, it's possible what I suggested to Evan is exactly why Rhys may have known Joan Cromer was a blonde." He snapped his fingers. "One last item: stop by the Events Unlimited office and ask Brenda if she noticed Joan paying special attention to Rhys at that conference last fall. And also, if Joan talked to her before coming to Pennsylvania about any plans to meet someone here."

"Roger that. Are you going to be at this number all day?"

"I'll make a point of it. I want to look through Lenny's books on psychiatry. I suspect Rhys Llewellyn may have a serious condition, and I might find some clues there."

He hung up the phone and turned to Garrett. "Now we wait to see what Jim comes up with."

Garrett nodded and glanced at his watch. "I hope Evan will sleep in today. He's stretched pretty thin."

"Agreed. He needs some time to himself at this point." Mal grinned wryly and finished his coffee. "Interesting how cousin Rhys coming to give Evan moral support has turned into 'how do we entertain cousin Rhys today?' Wonder what he did last night after the show when Evan told him he didn't want to go out and didn't invite him to come back here with us?"

"Could he have friends here? Carbondale isn't far."

"It's possible, but not likely," Mal said. "Augusta tells me people tend to be parochial here and seldom even visit nearby towns. A different world view from

177

living in a metropolitan area. And it also seems miners tend to stick with other miners."

"That's not so unusual. People whose profession is their entire life tend to do that. Cops among them. You're different."

"Yeah, mainly because of Augusta. But partly because I've always loved opera. I'll tell you, I don't discuss that at work and I listen to country western right along with my fellow detectives." He laughed. "Then I get in my car and blast the classical music station all the way home."

"Back up a minute," Garrett said. "About Rhys—it would be interesting to know who his friends are."

"It would be interesting to know if Rhys even has any friends. I don't think he fits in well with the mining community, for several reasons."

Milly and Augusta joined them, having come downstairs quietly. "Evan's still sound asleep," Augusta told them. "I peeked in his room. He's out."

"You went in his room?" Mal stared at his wife, feigning indignation.

She laughed. "I said I peeked in the door. I figured those beers would do the job. He was exhausted. He really needs some time to recharge."

"Where's Lenny, anyway?" Milly headed toward the kitchen. "If we're going to let Evan sleep, no bacon and eggs this morning. Fruit and pastries?"

"Len went to his favorite restaurant in Mountainhome. He's bringing back some breakfast sandwiches. He hoped you wouldn't be offended," Garrett chuckled.

"Can we take the phone off the hook?" Augusta asked. "Dollars to donuts Rhys will call at some point to see if Evan 'needs' him."

"Not a great idea. Jim Edmonds should be calling me back sometime later this morning. Let's turn the ringer down, though," Mal acted as he spoke.

They heard a car pull into the driveway. "Oh, good," Garrett said. "Lenny's back with breakfast." He stood. "At this point my gut feeling is that we need to keep the two men separated. Find some way to keep Rhys away from Evan."

The breakfast sandwiches hit the spot. Lenny entertained them with what he encountered at the Mountainhome Deli, abuzz with news of the murder.

"Lots of looks in my direction and conversations among people enjoying breakfast. Finally, one of them managed to ask me if I knew Evan." He laughed heartily. "It felt like the entire diner full of people were holding their breath waiting for my answer."

"And you told them...?" Augusta asked.

"I told them, 'I'm proud to say he's my house guest and a close friend of my niece Augusta's. And for the record, he didn't kill anybody.'"

"Oh, dear. Let's find a way to keep Evan here for the day. He doesn't need to hear about any of that," Augusta said.

She had an idea and phoned Emily Detweiler. "Can you and some other cast members keep Rhys busy? Evan is still asleep, and I think he needs today to regroup."

"Sure, we can do that. We entertained him last night. He likes hanging out with us. I seem to be the only one who thinks he's a jerk," Emily replied. "Is Evan all right?" Augusta heard the concern in her voice.

"He will be. This has been extremely stressful, and he's tried hard to focus on the show. He just needs sleep. And no Rhys."

"Aye, aye, Cap'n," Emily chuckled. "Keep me posted?"

"Absolutely." Augusta turned to her friends. "Well, I think the *Carousel* cast will keep Rhys occupied today. And tonight as well, if necessary."

She peeked into Evan's room again after she went upstairs. He was still sleeping peacefully; so far as she could tell, he hadn't moved. *Interesting comment last night about singing "Sixteen Tons" for his daddy. He never talks much about his father. He told me once Dylan Llewellyn was somehow badly injured in a mining accident, but at least he survived.*

The phone rang about 9:30; Jim calling back with his report.

"No luck about Joan mentioning Rhys to the Cromers, but I struck gold on a couple of other things. First of all, yes, Joan showed her mother a bracelet she claimed Evan gave her. A gold charm bracelet with a heart charm—you know, the kind that opens and has two pictures in it. She said the pictures were of Evan and Joan. She looked through Joan's jewelry and said it wasn't there."

"Good work, Detective. You said a couple of things?" Mal made notes on his pad as the two men talked.

"This is even better. You remember that framed photo on the table next to Joan's bed? The one she had an artificial flower twined around…a snapshot of her and Evan that looked like it was taken in a bar? Maybe a hotel lounge, by the photographer there."

"Yeah, I recall seeing that."

Garrett and Augusta waited expectantly as they watched Mal rapidly taking notes.

"After you told me about Rhys resembling Evan, I took a closer look at that photo and I don't think it's Evan. The man in the photo is exchanging googly eyes with Joan and his hair and eyes appear to be darker than Evan's. I think it might be Rhys. I borrowed the photo and forensics is working on it now to enlarge and enhance it. I'm betting there will be something about the face that's different from Evan's…hairline, length of chin, something. We have a number of Evan's professional headshots and it'll be easy to compare."

"It should be." Mal grinned broadly and gave his audience a thumbs up. "Great work, Detective Edmonds. I owe you lunch when I get back to Cincinnati. No, dinner."

"I'll hold you to that, partner. Oh, and remember you mentioned Rhys's state of mind? That he might have some kind of mental illness? Well, I think we all are aware Joan certainly did. Mrs. Cromer decided to tell me that Joan had seen a psychiatrist a few times, beginning when she was in high school. She gave me the name and phone number and said she'd contacted this guy…" a pause while he consulted his notes…"Dr. Aaron

Fielding, and gave him permission to answer any questions I had."

"Interesting that she chose to let you know about Joan's mental issues. It's hard to know at this point if that might be helpful, but obviously she trusts you. Always a good thing."

"No luck at Events Unlimited, though," Jim told him. "Brenda doesn't recall Joan being especially attentive to any of the attendees during that conference in October. And she never mentioned to them exactly why she was coming to Pennsylvania."

"Well, the picture may very well be proof positive that Joan and Rhys not only knew each other, but were in a relationship at one time. When will you be able to take another look at it?"

"Hopefully, later today. If not, tomorrow morning."

"Great. Talk to you again soon."

Malcolm repeated the gist of the conversation to Augusta and Garrett. "If the photo shows that the man with Joan is not Evan but could be Rhys, we might have him."

"On the other hand, all that will prove is that Rhys and Joan knew each other," Augusta speculated. "It still doesn't provide motive. We don't know when that photo was taken—we're just guessing it may have been last October. Another thing, how would Rhys have known Joan would be at the Playhouse last Wednesday night?"

Garrett chimed in, "We've learned Rhys knew Joan had been pursuing Evan, because Evan told him about it. For whatever reason, it's possible Rhys showed up at the theater on Wednesday night and killed her. Definitely a crime of passion. Then he fled back to Carbondale. I find it surprising he didn't leave the state. But we are all in agreement Rhys is behaving erratically."

"When he saw in the newspapers that Evan was suspected of the murder, Rhys decided to show up, ostensibly to offer his cousin moral support," Mal concluded. "Why is he continuing to hang around, though?"

"Well, for one thing he has no clue we're aware he crossed paths with Joan last fall," Augusta remarked.

"I have to talk to George LaBar," Mal said. "He needs to know what we've learned so far, and especially our suspicions about the photo."

"You know what Evan said to me after that article came out in *The Pocono Record*?" Augusta asked. "He said somebody had set him up for Joan's murder. Is there any way Rhys could have actually done that?"

Malcolm stared hard at each of them. "That might be why Rhys is hanging around. He may be looking for a way to further implicate Evan in Joan's death."

Chapter 14
Rhys and Joan

"Len and I are headed out for provisions. What are you reading?"

Augusta, curled up in a chair in Len's library, lifted the book to show Milly the title, *An Introduction to Diseases of the Mind.*

"Good Lord, Augusta." Milly frowned. "Now isn't a good time to start playing amateur shrink."

"I'm not. I just want to see if I can get some insight into Rhys's thought processes."

"That sure sounds like playing amateur shrink to me," Milly remarked. "Well, I know there's no stopping you. Just remember this is a topic you really don't know anything about."

The house grew pleasantly quiet. Malcolm and Garrett had gone out earlier, so Augusta continued to read uninterrupted.

In the clearest case of the depressed phase, the patient is suicidal and homicidal in a few situations (this can result in homicide followed by suicide). In these scenarios, institutional commitment is in order and indicated. In other situations, the depression has led to an inability of the patient to work, eat, and function; hospitalization is also indicated in these cases...

Augusta inserted a bookmark and laid the book aside as she heard Evan heading downstairs. "Let me get you something to eat," she offered.

"Why didn't someone wake me up?"

"We all figured you needed sleep."

"I guess I must have," he admitted. "I don't remember the last time I slept so long." He followed Augusta into the kitchen.

"Yes, eleven hours is a long stretch. Eggs and bacon? Fruit?" She busied herself at the refrigerator.

"All the above," Evan laughed. "But I can cook for myself. Why not just keep me company? And then I think I'll go for a walk."

He glanced around. "Where is everybody, anyway?"

"Out running errands. Milly and Len are grocery shopping, and Garrett went to Mt. Pocono with Mal. He needed to talk to George LaBar."

"Ah, Trooper LaBar. Not my favorite person these days." Evan cracked four eggs and scrambled them vigorously with a wire whisk.

'He's not your enemy, Evan. He's just doing his job." Augusta pulled a bowl of fruit from the refrigerator.

"I know that. He has a murderer to find and arrest. Unfortunately, that's what I think he sees when he looks at me."

"You might be surprised." She sliced fruit—melons, grapes, and peaches—and mixed them in a bowl, helping herself to a small serving as she sat at the kitchen island. "Oh, and there's a fresh pot of coffee. Milly put it on just before she left."

Augusta poured herself a cup. "You really intrigued me last night when you mentioned your father. I think you said your parents have tickets for the show on Friday?"

"Yes. And a few other family members and close friends are coming as well. You know, Augusta, my people love music. Maybe not opera, but I think they'll like this show." He grabbed two pieces of toast as they popped up.

Augusta lifted an eyebrow and Evan laughed. "I need carbs."

She pulled the butter dish from the refrigerator as she said, "How long has your family been in Northeastern Pennsylvania anyway? I know many miners immigrated from Europe when coal was discovered here."

Evan scooped some fruit into a bowl, settled himself across from Augusta, and dug into his brunch. "My family came here from Wales in 1832. So there have been Llewellyns in this region for many generations."

Augusta stirred cream and sugar into her coffee. "The Welsh certainly have a strong musical tradition."

"Did you know the very first *eisteddfod* in the United States took place in Carbondale in 1850?"

"No, I wasn't aware of that. A festival of music and poetry, correct?"

"*Da iawn*," he grinned as he spoke. "That means 'well done.'"

"You speak Welsh?" Augusta stared at him.

"Not really," Evan laughed. "Words to some songs and a few common phrases. I think I'd like to learn, though." He took a few more bites of scrambled egg. "That's my heritage, Augusta. My proud heritage— mining and music. Two things my people are very good at."

"Your father was disabled in a mining accident, if I remember correctly—his left arm?"

"Yes. Shattered when part of a ceiling collapsed. He's never been able to use it since, and that happened when I was a senior in high school." Evan stirred coffee as he gazed back into the past. "That was the same year I won first prize in the *eisteddfod*. The year my teacher took me to Temple University to audition for the music program. I received a full scholarship."

"You had a difficult choice to make, I believe," Augusta said softly.

"No, actually, that wasn't an issue. The company found an office position for my father. We were among the fortunate. We owned our home and everything in it. We even had two cars—both of them used, of course. My mother was an elementary school teacher. There was never any expectation for me to go into the mine."

"You never told me about that." Augusta studied Evan, recalling their time together. *He's different now— more confident. Back then, he needed constant reassurance. I don't believe he was in love with me, despite his declarations. I can't deny the chemistry, though.*

Evan traced a pattern in the wood on the table with the handle of his spoon. "My daddy never actively opposed my choice of career. That was Rhys's father, my Uncle Dave. I told you they were twins?"

"Yes, last night."

"My father was the second-born. He was a gentle soul. A strong man in many ways, but kind, a loving husband and father."

"And your Uncle David was not."

"He wasn't unkind. But like most miners, he had certain expectations of his family."

"You know, you've never mentioned Rhys's romantic involvements. He never married?"

"He's had plenty of female attention, but as far as I know, nothing serious. I'm not sure why. He always seemed to be focused on some project. And then he went through that period where he seemed…lost. For a time, I wasn't sure he was going to get to New York for my Met debut. But he was there."

Evan's eyes brightened. "You can't imagine what a thrill it was for me to bring some of my family members to New York for that occasion. They were all proud. But it was my dad's smile after the performance that meant the most."

He glanced at Augusta as she flicked away a tear. "Something in your eye?"

"No. Something in my heart. That's a beautiful tribute, Evan. I'll look forward to meeting Dylan Llewellyn."

***

"Here's the thing," Mal said to George LaBar. "This amplified photo that my partner will see soon may be proof that Rhys Llewellyn and Joan Cromer were involved, most likely late last fall. And we can arrange to get it up here pronto once Jim's had a good look at it."

"Lots of interesting stuff here, Malcolm." George sat back and linked his fingers behind his head. "My first inclination was to get in touch with Rhys and ask him to come in so we could talk, but having that photo in our hands by sometime tomorrow makes me feel we should hold off. I don't see any reason to suspect another murder could happen. Joan's death was personal. The fact Rhys is staying at a resort makes me think he feels pretty sure we don't suspect him. We'll sit on him, though. Make sure he doesn't start loading suitcases into his car. You say he's staying at Skytop? That's pretty pricey."

"Yes. It struck both my wife and me as odd that he's not just driving back and forth between here and Carbondale, unless he has another reason for staying close to Evan."

"And your wife has come up with the idea Rhys may be looking to implicate Evan in Joan's murder. How much of this is Evan aware of, anyhow?"

"We haven't told him any of this as yet. I wanted to talk to you first. Evan suspects something is wrong where Rhys is concerned, but it's just a gut feeling. He doesn't yet know about the conference in Cincinnati, where it looks more and more as if Rhys and Joan not only crossed paths, but got together."

"You say the cousins were close as youngsters."

"Yeah, according to Evan, Rhys taught him to fight. And was his champion when he was bullied. It's hard to believe when you see him now, but apparently Evan was a scrawny kid in glasses when he was a young teen."

"Do you have any idea as to how to find out where Rhys was the night Joan was murdered?"

Malcolm leaned forward. "He didn't show up here until two days ago. Evan told us Rhys phoned him Sunday to let him know he was coming to stay a few days. That's another thing that doesn't seem to fit. There's been plenty of publicity in all the newspapers in this area about Evan performing at Pocono Playhouse for these two weeks, starting on June 6."

"Well, it's possible he was out of town or tied up with his project. Maybe he's been in meetings with the Big Plains Mining Company. If he's been tied up nights that would explain him not showing up here until June 13." George leaned forward and made a note to himself. "I'll make some calls and see what I can find out. Joan was murdered last Wednesday, June 8."

"Rhys called Evan on Sunday, June 12, four days after the murder. Rhys must have read in the papers on Friday, June 10, that Evan was a suspect. He waited a couple of days before he called his cousin. No state troopers at his door, so he was sure nobody suspected him."

"Nobody here in Monroe County knew him, and his name never came up. Augusta noticed the physical resemblance between the two men the day she met him, correct?"

"Yes, and we've recently learned their fathers were twins." Malcolm sat back, engrossed in their theorizing, enjoying it immensely. *This is why I became a homicide detective.* "Then Augusta found out about the conference in Cincinnati. Joan had pursued Evan to Atlanta in September. Rhys and Joan may have met and had some kind of relationship the next month. Only Rhys never told his cousin about that. Why?"

"Or, at least, that's what Evan told you. No way to prove that Rhys said nothing to his cousin about meeting Miss Cromer."

"That's true. My gut feeling is that Evan is being straight with us, but you have a point."

George leaned forward. "Well, I'll let you know if I can find out anything about Rhys's whereabouts on the night of June 8. It's entirely possible he was in Barrett Township that night."

"And he spotted Joan in the Playhouse parking lot and killed her, for whatever reason. What could have put him in such a state of rage?" Mal gazed into the distance for a moment. "I sat with Rhys last night at the *Carousel* performance. We talked before the show and during intermission, and most of the time he seemed perfectly normal. But he made a couple of comments...Rhys may be mentally unstable, George. I know Evan thinks that as well."

"Well, that's why they're called 'crimes of passion.' If he's already dealing with emotional problems that indicates he'd be more apt to snap."

"There's this…in the show, Billy Bigelow—the character Evan plays—falls on his knife so he can avoid being arrested. I could see Rhys's face during that scene, and his reaction was totally unlike that of most of the audience."

"He was smiling," LaBar ventured.

Mal shook his head. "Drumming his fingers on the arm of his chair. Staring at the ceiling." He stood. "I don't believe the Llewellyn cousins have spoken since last night. The cast members have been keeping Rhys entertained and I'm sure they can continue to do that. Of course, they know nothing about any of this. They just think he's cool because he's Evan's cousin and he likes hanging out with them."

"Can I get a ticket for the show tonight? Might be a good idea for me to be on hand."

"Well, they say they're sold out, but management always holds back a few tickets for friends." Malcolm smiled. "I know a lady in the cast who can probably get one for you."

***

Erotomania. A rare mental disorder in which a person (often a woman) is fixated on the idea another person, someone they may never have met and often a celebrity, is in love with them. Also called de Clérambault

193

syndrome, erotomania is rare. It can happen on its own. But it's usually linked to another mental health condition, such as schizophrenia or manic-depression. It can last for weeks or years.

Erotomania seems to be a little more common in women. But some studies show men are just as likely to get it. The condition can show up after puberty, but it usually happens around midlife or later.

Genetics may have something to do with erotomania if delusional disorders are in the patient's family history. Environment, lifestyle, and overall mental health also play a role. Common traits of people with erotomania can include low self-esteem; a feeling of rejection or loneliness; social isolation.

Augusta put a marker in the book and considered what she'd just learned.

'A feeling of rejection or loneliness; social isolation.' How would that apply to Joan? Did something happen to her when she was a child that made her feel that way?

She picked up the phone and dialed the Cincinnati Homicide Headquarters and asked to speak with Detective Edmonds if he were available. She was in luck; Jim was in the office.

"This is Detective Edmonds."

"Hi, Jim. It's Augusta. Mal is meeting with George LaBar even as we speak, but I was hoping you'd have a few minutes to answer a couple of questions I have."

"Sure. Ask away."

"Did you see any photos of Joan? Other than the one of her with a man we now think must be Rhys Llewellyn. Or maybe even a portrait of her at the Cromer home?"

"As a matter of fact, there was a framed photographic portrait of her in the family's living room. She was an attractive woman."

Augusta glanced again at the book in her hand. "I was just researching what might be Joan's condition—something called 'erotomania'—and had one specific question in mind: it's hard for me to understand why an obviously intelligent and attractive woman could become so fixated on someone she barely knew."

"I've thought the same thing," Jim responded. "I doubt Evan had a clue what would come of what he considered a casual weekend with her. What, two nights?"

"Yes. And I believe him when he says he told her it was exactly that, a casual weekend."

"Well…what a guy says and what a woman hears often don't line up. And vice versa."

"True, but not to that extent." She hesitated. "You said Mrs. Cromer gave you permission to talk to Joan's psychiatrist. He might have the answers to our questions."

Jim gave a low whistle. "That's a tough one, Augusta. You want me to ask her shrink?"

"It might help explain her mental state."

"I don't know if it's going to help us find her killer."

"Probably not. On the other hand, it might help if we understood her better. What a tragic end for this lady. No matter what she did to Evan, he certainly didn't wish for this to happen to her."

"Roger that. I'll get back to you."

Augusta replaced the handset on the phone, her fingers lingering for a moment.

Joan believed herself to be in love with Evan. Rhys may have thought he was in love with Joan.

When did she tell him about her obsession with Evan?

***

"We have something we must discuss with you, Evan, and it won't be easy to hear." Mal, Garrett, and Augusta were seated in the library with Evan.

He looked startled. "Something about Joan's murder?"

"When you told Rhys about Joan last Christmas, what did he say? We really need to know about any remarks he may have made." Mal leaned toward Evan as he spoke.

Evan frowned. "Mainly, he just listened. I don't remember him saying much of anything."

"The least comment he might have made about her. About what she was doing to you," Garrett added.

"I did most of the talking. Maybe all of it. I told him the whole story, from spending that weekend in Indianapolis to her showing up in Atlanta in September. I'd hoped that would be the end of it, but as you know, she showed up again a couple of times after that. I told him about those the other day when he came down and checked into Skytop."

"He must have made some kind of comment about her continuing to pursue you," Mal remarked.

"You know, it struck me as kind of odd that he didn't say anything when I told him about that. And about her showing up here." Evan shifted uneasily in his chair. "Where are you going with this, Mal?"

Malcolm gazed at Augusta, who picked up the narrative. "Evan—this is going to be difficult for you to hear, as Mal said. We have reason to believe that Rhys met Joan in Cincinnati in October, and they may have had a relationship."

Evan stared from one of them to the other, his face a study in confusion and dismay. "What the hell? Are you sitting here telling me Rhys may have been the person who strangled Joan?"

"We don't know that yet," Mal replied. "But there may be proof that at the very least they were involved. When you were in Indianapolis, did you and Joan have a photo taken together? Maybe in a hotel lounge?"

"God, no. We spent our time together in her hotel room. We weren't staying in the same hotel, and we never even took a meal in a restaurant, just room service."

Mal glanced at Augusta and Garrett. "That pretty much clinches it, then." He turned to Evan. "My partner Jim Edmonds and I were in Joan's apartment in her parents' home in Cincinnati. One entire wall was covered with photographs of you...."

197

"I don't want to hear this," Evan interrupted, dismissively gesturing at them as he stood abruptly and walked to the door. "It's sickening."

"I understand, but you need to know these things." Mal gave Evan a moment to return to his chair before he continued. "On her bedside table we found a photo of Joan and a man we thought was you. But my partner Jim went back this morning and looked more closely, and he now believes it's a photo of Joan and Rhys, gazing at each other as if they are smitten. He says the man in the photo resembles you strongly, but his coloring is darker. It's a small picture, just a snapshot. Quite possibly taken by a hotel lounge or nightclub photographer. The photo is presently being enlarged and enhanced, and I'm betting it's a picture of Joan and Rhys, taken in October in Cincinnati. There may well be a time stamp on the back, or some other identification which will prove exactly when and where it was taken."

"If Rhys met Joan and fell in love with her…then learned from you about her obsession…." Augusta didn't complete her sentence.

"We don't know what happened during the intervening months, of course," Mal said. "My partner and I found no evidence of any of this, and Joan's mother didn't recall Joan ever talking about Rhys. So this is speculation," he concluded. "Yet Rhys definitely becomes a suspect in Joan's murder. Jealousy is a strong motive. For whatever reason, it's possible Rhys came to the Playhouse last Wednesday night, found Joan while she was placing that note on your windshield, confronted her and killed her."

Evan sank back in his chair, head in hands. "Oh, dear God…." he moaned. He looked up at Mal, stricken. "Could I have somehow prevented this?"

"You knew nothing about what passed between them. You weren't even aware Rhys had ever met Joan."

"Until he mentioned her blond hair. Asked me to describe how she died." He took a long, deep breath. "He's sick, Mal. He's mentally ill; I'm convinced of it. If he killed her, he couldn't have meant to."

Augusta, Mal, and Garrett exchanged glances. "I believe you could be right about him being emotionally disturbed," Malcolm said. "Something seems very wrong. Those intense mood swings. When he first got here, the frantic non-stop talking about what is most likely a hopeless attempt to revive the Conowingo Tunnel Project. Then you described what happened yesterday…cheating at golf, asking questions about Joan's death. Almost like a different person."

"It wasn't just that he was asking questions about Joan's death. It's…he *demanded* I tell him. As if he *had* to know how she died." Again, Evan's face sank into his hands. "You were right. This is…almost impossible to hear. And to bear." He choked on the last word.

Augusta moved to sit next to him, placing a sympathetic hand on his shoulder. "Of course it is. We understand. Your cousin was your champion when you were young. Try to hold onto that—and remember, we all agree he could be seriously ill."

"Which could make him dangerous until we can pick him up and question him," Mal added. "Trooper LaBar agreed to wait until the photo arrives from the

Cincinnati Police Department, which will be either later tonight or sometime tomorrow."

"In the meantime," Garrett said, "you have to stay away from him. Emily has been orchestrating that." A look at Evan's face prompted him to add, "No, she isn't aware of any of this. She's an intuitive young woman, though, and senses something is wrong with Rhys. She told Augusta that on Monday when they had brunch together."

"I hate this. I love my cousin, but I can't deny something is very wrong. I don't like to think of Emily being around him." Evan heaved a sigh.

"She's not by herself. A group of cast members is keeping him entertained," Augusta told him.

"George LaBar wants to come to the performance tonight," Mal said to Augusta. "Can you get him a ticket?"

"Oh, good. I'm sure I can," Augusta replied, feeling a definite sense of relief.

"So for now, we wait," Mal told them. He turned to Evan. "Sorry, but I have to ask this: do you know if Rhys owns a gun?"

"He might. We all learned to shoot when we were kids. It would make sense for him to have one since he travels all over the country by himself."

Evan covered his eyes with his hand. "I know what you're asking. Is he carrying? Who the hell knows?" A short, sharp laugh.

"And now, I have to prepare myself to perform Billy Bigelow once again and somehow put all this out of my mind." He glanced around the room. "Anybody have any suggestions?"

The room grew silent as they listened to the ticking of the century clock on the mantle.

Evan stared at Mal. "This is going to end badly, isn't it?"

Susan Moore Jordan

Chapter 15
Carousel with a Twist

Mal hung up the phone and turned to Augusta.

"It's official. The man in the photo with Joan Cromer is definitely not Evan Llewellyn, though he strongly resembles Evan. It has to be Rhys. The picture is now in the hands of the Ohio State Police who will deliver it to a PSP trooper at the state border. It will then be relayed to the Mt. Pocono barracks and should be in their hands between 9:00 and 10:00 this evening. I'm going to run back over to Mt. Pocono and give this information to George so he can have it brought to the theater as soon as it arrives. With any luck, we may even get it before the performance of *Carousel* ends tonight."

Milly came into the library from the kitchen. "Dinner at 5:30. Salads, mostly, because Augusta and Evan don't like a heavy meal before they perform. Evan's napping again but asked me to wake him by 5:00."

Mal nodded as he headed for the front door. "That's fine. I won't be long."

No sooner had he driven away than the phone rang again. Augusta picked it up.

"Hi, Augusta. Is Mal still there?" Jim Edmonds' voice.

"You just missed him. He left about five minutes ago. You could probably catch him at Trooper LaBar's office."

"I'll see if I can do that. You might be interested in this. Just got off the phone with Mrs. Cromer. It seems she found something of interest while cleaning out drawers in Joan's room—a letter from Rhys. Joan had it tucked in the back of a drawer. I'm kind of surprised she kept it."

Augusta clutched the phone. "Oh, my goodness. Do you have any idea what was in it?"

"As a matter of fact, she read it to me. Not lengthy, and I made some notes."

"Hold on a second while I get something to write this down," Augusta picked up the pad next to the phone along with a pen. "Okay, shoot."

Jim continued, "No envelope and no date, the letter begins 'To my dearest love' and begs her to see him again. 'My life is meaningless without you,' was one thing he said."

Augusta scribbled furiously. "Jim, you know Joan wrote a bunch of letters to herself and signed Evan's name to them. Could this be the same kind of thing?"

"I saw those, and we have copies on file. Mrs. Cromer says the handwriting is different on this one. It was Evan she was obsessed with. Why would she write a letter to herself from a guy she dumped?"

"Maybe her psychiatrist could answer that. But you're right, this sounds important."

"I'll arrange to have it sent to Pennsylvania pronto. Oh, one more thing Rhys said in the letter, something about how he couldn't understand her fixation on Evan. 'I'm twice the man he is. You'd know that if you'd known him when he was young.' And Evan says Rhys never even mentioned Joan to him?"

"No, he did not." Augusta read over her notes. "You know, I believe that's an actual letter from Rhys; Joan didn't write it. Do you have George LaBar's number?"

"Yeah, I do. Sounds as if maybe you're closing in on your killer. Wish I could be there for the finale."

"You've been a key player, Jim. I'm sure Mal wishes you were here."

"Oh, Augusta?"

"Yes?"

"Try to stay out of the line of fire, will you? Just saying."

She smiled. "Of course I will. Talk to you soon."

Augusta's mind churned with this new information. *Well, what a stroke of luck. No doubt proof positive of Rhys and Joan being involved...and a motive for murder.*

She checked her watch. *It's only four. There's something I think I should do.* "I have an errand to run," she told Milly. "I'll be back for dinner."

"Hold on, Augusta." Milly caught Augusta's arm. "Exactly where are you headed? I don't like your tone of voice. You've got something brewing you probably shouldn't have."

"I just want to talk to Rhys for a few minutes."

Milly folded her arms across her chest. "I was right. Something you absolutely should not do. You'll tip him off."

"No, I won't. I just want to remind him how much his cousin cares for him."

"And you want to do this because...?"

"Evan said something I can't get out of my head. 'I love my cousin, but I can't deny something is very wrong.' Rhys isn't able to think straight at all. He needs to consider what this situation is doing to the cousin he loves."

"Mal is not going to like this," Milly mumbled. "And I don't like it either."

"I'll just tell Rhys why Evan hasn't been in touch with him today. He's exhausted by what he's dealing with, being a suspect...the only suspect...in Joan's murder, and having to perform every night despite that."

"I hope to hell you know what you're doing, Augusta."

On her drive to Skytop, Augusta attempted to put her thoughts in order. *Just remind Rhys that Evan still sees him as his champion. His hero. Maybe in Rhys's shattered mind that will get through, and he'll realize he somehow needs to step up. I know it's a long shot, but it's worth a try.*

Life can be unbelievably strange, she mused. *At one time Evan thought he was in love with me. Joan became obsessed with Evan. Rhys had a relationship with Joan and I'm betting she dumped him, and told him why—because he wasn't Evan. That's what prompted his comment in the letter Rhys wrote her, "I'm twice the man he is."*

***

As she had thought she might, Augusta spotted Rhys in the Tap Room. It surprised her to see him not at the bar, but seated at a table drinking coffee.

"May I join you?" She sat opposite him as she spoke, noting the place setting in front of him. "Late brunch?"

"Yeah. I guess I overdid it last night." He lifted an eyebrow at her. "What brings you to Skytop, Professor McKee? Or should I say Mrs. Mitchell?"

"Either works," she replied. "Maybe you're just tired?"

Rhys stared at her but didn't comment. She noted the drooping shoulders, unkempt hair, the pinched mouth.

"I came to see you," Augusta said quietly. "You and I haven't really had much of a chance to talk."

"Do we have anything to talk about?" The words were clipped.

Well, he's not going to be easy to reach. He seems to be deeply depressed. Such a difference from the Rhys I first met.

"We do. Your cousin Evan." She took a deep breath. "You know, when I first met Evan, he talked about you quite a bit. How important you were in his life. All the

207

things you did for him when he was a kid. None of that has changed, Rhys. You still mean a great deal to him."

Rhys took a swallow of coffee as he gazed sullenly at Augusta.

"Evan is in the midst of the greatest crisis of his life right now," she continued. "Suspected of murdering a woman he barely knew—Joan Cromer."

Augusta noted his reaction to the name: a slight flicker in his eyes.

"And still, he's continuing to perform in this intense role he feels so deeply. You know what he told me? He likes playing Billy because he can relate to the character. He says it reminds him of some of the hard times he experienced as a kid. Hard times you helped him get through."

Rhys glanced off into the distance, and Augusta sensed a slight change in his attitude.

"He said that about me? That I was important to him?"

"Yes, he told me all about you when I first met him in New York. It meant a lot when you called to say you were coming to stay for a few days."

A glimmer of a smile. "I'm sure it's hard to imagine when you see the man he's become, but he was a pitiful kid. Skinny, awkward, scared."

"He owes you a lot, Rhys. And he knows that. I know Evan hasn't been in touch with you since yesterday," she added. "But it's mainly because he's slept nearly the entire day. He was exhausted."

She leaned toward him. "Maybe you're feeling the same. It's hard work to cheer someone up who's going through a crisis. Being suspected of murdering a woman he felt sorry for."

Another flicker in his eyes. *Okay, Augusta, you've said your piece. Maybe you've said too much.*

"Well, I'll leave you to enjoy your food. Milly has the tickets for tonight, look for her."

"Thanks." As she stood Rhys caught her wrist, and the way he gripped it was unsettling. "I'd like to talk more sometime." She couldn't read his expression.

"We'll definitely do that."

He abruptly released her arm, and she managed to refrain from rubbing it. When she was out of his sight Augusta looked down and saw the ugly red marks made by his fingers.

***

"Good God, Augusta. I can't believe you." Mal managed to control his anger, but sitting on the bed in their room, Augusta felt a little like a child being reprimanded.

"I was with him for maybe fifteen minutes, and here is exactly what I said to him." She relayed their conversation as closely as she could recall it. "Yes, I mentioned Joan. I referred to her as a woman Evan barely knew but felt sorry for. He didn't give me much of a reaction." *Should I tell him about how Rhys clutched my arm? Probably not.*

"I know you've been reading the same book I have from Len's library, and I take it you think he could be suffering from some form of mental illness. Frankly, I agree it's a possibility. It would explain a lot. It's a good thing you kept quiet about the letter Mrs. Cromer found."

"Why would I have told him about that?" Augusta asked. "That's your proof, isn't it? I'd think when you get it tomorrow you might have enough to charge him."

"Not necessarily. I can't believe Jim read that letter to you. What the hell was he thinking?"

"Maybe he figured you'd tell me anyway?"

"You can bet he'll get an earful about that gaffe." Mal shook his head. "First we have to prove Rhys wrote it. If he did, it's certainly a strong clue and will reinforce George's interview with him. You said you were hoping to remind him what's happening to the cousin he once loved. What were you really after? A confession?"

"I hardly expected that as the result of a brief conversation. Maybe he'll be able to think at least a little more rationally, though."

"You're not a psychiatrist, Gus." Mal stood and faced her. "You have no clue what's going on in that man's head. And we're all pretty much convinced he just murdered a woman he may have been in love with. About a one-eighty from rational thought, wouldn't you agree?"

"Yes, I know that's all true. Maybe it was a mistake, but I felt compelled to try to get through to him."

Mal folded his arms over his chest. "Because you wanted to do something for Evan."

"I wanted to do something that might help solve this case. We all know Evan didn't murder Joan. It's beginning to look more and more as if Rhys did."

Milly's voice floated up the stairs. "Dinner, everybody!"

Mal lifted Augusta to her feet and wrapped strong arms around her. "I never want you to be in danger again, Gus." She heard the roughness in his voice. "It's happened far too often."

Augusta returned the embrace. "I know that. I honestly don't believe what I said to him could put me in danger, Mal."

***

Mal met George in the parking lot and handed him the ticket to *Carousel*, telling him quickly about the letter Mrs. Cromer had discovered and what Jim had relayed about its contents.

"That could be the proof we need," LaBar said.

He waved a hand at the edge of the parking lot. "I see Rhys is already here. That green and white Dodge is his car."

Once inside the Playhouse, Mal found his aisle seat on the audience right side of the center section. He could see Rhys and Len on the side section on the left, three rows from the front, Rhys in an aisle seat. George LaBar was in the third row from the back in the center section on the same aisle as Rhys, an anonymous theatergoer so far as Rhys was concerned, while George was well aware of where Rhys was seated. Mal observed him glancing at Rhys frequently as he seemed to be studying his playbill. Garrett and Milly were seated in the side section to Malcolm's right, near the back.

The overture began, and Mal's attention was split between the performance on the stage and making sure Rhys stayed put. Rhys seemed to be engrossed in the show.

Mal was still somewhat perturbed, thinking about Augusta's impromptu visit to Skytop Lodge to talk to Rhys. It sounded harmless enough as she described it, but Rhys was a loose cannon. Augusta didn't seem to understand how volatile he might become, and how quickly that could happen.

Once again Malcolm was impressed with Evan's focused performance. No one in the audience except his friends would have known the stress he'd been under for the past week. He never broke character; he sang magnificently in the "bench scene" and his performance of the "Soliloquy" stopped the show.

Malcolm genuinely liked Evan. He had liked *Inspecteur* Jean-Luc Marchand when their paths crossed in Paris as they worked together on the murder of a violinist from Cincinnati. *Augusta's old beaus are quality people*, he thought with a grin. *I hope I don't meet any more of them, though. Two is more than enough.*

He settled back and enjoyed Augusta's first big number, "June Is Bustin' Out All Over," still keeping one eye on Rhys. He loved that the choreographer had included Augusta as Nettie in the dance, even giving her a brief solo, which brought hearty applause from the audience. *My lady can still dance*, he thought. *One of the first things I loved about her all those years ago when I saw her in Carmen.*

The "Soliloquy" and a short reprise of "June" brought the first act to a close. Mal wandered down the aisle to the front of the theater, glancing into the orchestra pit, while watching Rhys out of the corner of his eye. Rhys was deep in conversation with Len and so was occupied for the present.

Mal walked back up the aisle, strolled through the vestibule and went outside briefly where he spotted George LaBar, who gave him a slight nod. The PSP was charged with collecting the photo from the Ohio State Police at the border, and the plan was to relay it to George here at the Playhouse so it would be in his hands as soon as possible. Mal and George planned to detain Rhys quietly and take him to the Mt. Pocono barracks for questioning immediately after the performance.

The audience returned and settled in their seats, the lights dimmed, and the show continued with a big ensemble number, "This Was a Real Nice Clambake." Mal saw it as filler, but Gus told him the cast loved performing it. It was a light, happy beginning to the second act. A comedy scene with Julie's friend Carrie Pipperidge and Jigger Craigin, the bad guy, followed, after which Act Two became increasingly dark. Evan as Billy left with Jigger to commit robbery, and Emily— who was a beautiful Julie—sang "What's the Use of Wonderin'" so poignantly Mal felt tears sting his eyes.

The failed robbery attempt ended with Billy falling on his knife to avoid going to jail, dying in Julie's arms. Malcolm had to remind himself to keep an eye on Rhys when Augusta sang "You'll Never Walk Alone." Listening to her, he felt a tear or two escape. *Augusta talked about Evan singing with such heartfelt emotion. It's exactly what she does, and always has. It's her gift.*

In the second act, the Heavenly Starkeeper briefly brought Billy back to Earth to see the child he never knew—his unhappy fifteen-year-old daughter, Louise. Billy was able to bring her some comfort. And before going back, Billy whispered in Julie's ear that he had always loved her, words he had never said to her in life.

Suddenly Mal sensed movement behind him and realized George LaBar had left his seat. He eased out of his own and walked quickly and quietly up the aisle to the vestibule, where he found George closely examining a photo. It was unmistakably Rhys with Joan.

The two men considered their best move. "The show is almost over," Mal told George. "There's a very short dialogue scene and the entire cast sings the end of 'You'll Never Walk Alone.' Maybe six or seven minutes tops. Why not wait until the final curtain and we can go down the aisle and try to hustle Rhys out quickly through the emergency exit without being too disruptive?"

George instructed the trooper who had delivered the photo to wait just outside the front door to the theater for them. He and Mal quietly re-entered the theater to wait at the rear of the auditorium, prepared to carry out their plan.

But Rhys Llewellyn was no longer in his seat. Neither was Len.

Mal quickly looked up toward the stage and saw an empty space where Augusta should have been.

Chapter 16
Back to the Past

George LaBar immediately turned and ran through the vestibule, Malcolm at his heels. George motioned to the trooper who was waiting outside to come with them and the three men ran along the outside of the building, headed toward the emergency exits, one for the audience and the other for backstage.

They found Len lying on the ground just feet from the first exit, struggling to pull himself up on an elbow. George motioned to his fellow trooper to take care of Len.

When Len saw Mal hesitate for an instant, he waved him off. "Go, go. I'll be okay. I think Rhys could be after Augusta."

"I'll check the parking lot," George told Malcolm. "You go backstage. I'll meet you there."

Mal nodded and ducked back inside the building, heading first for Augusta's dressing room near the rear of the backstage area. *I'm sure they are long gone.* He yanked open the door.

A first quick look around the room showed nothing seemed to be out of place. Augusta obviously was still in costume. Her street clothes were hanging on the back of the door—the blue dress he had helped her pick out before she left Cincinnati. Mal's throat tightened and he felt a catch in his chest when he saw her stilettos carefully placed side by side next to her dressing table.

Then he saw her wig on the floor, and realized with a flash of anger that Rhys must have snatched it from her head and thrown it down. He glanced over the items on the table and noticed immediately something that shouldn't have been there.

A streak of white ending in an arrow.

Mal knew little about stage makeup, but he was aware stage performers sometimes emphasized certain features by adding lighter or darker colors to their base makeup. It appeared that Augusta had managed to take a stick of white makeup with her and had marked the dressing table as a sign. It amazed Malcolm she had the presence of mind in what had to be a situation where she was threatened, most likely with a gun or a knife, to still find a way to communicate with him.

He moved swiftly from her dressing room to the backstage area. As Mal stood watching the action on the stage, he felt a rush of air as George came up behind him.

"Rhys's car is still in the parking lot. He planned this; he must have another one parked nearby," George hissed between gritted teeth.

Mal turned to him. "He has Augusta."

The two men, itching to pursue Rhys, watched impatiently as Evan spoke his final line of the evening and came offstage, a look of surprise and relief on his face when he saw the two men. The three of them quickly moved into the hallway as Evan said, "Rhys has taken Augusta, hasn't he?" Mal nodded. "I know where he's taking her," Evan said, his voice unsteady. "He's got a head start. We have to leave right now."

"Where are we headed, Evan?" George asked.

"Carbondale. Salem Mountain. An abandoned mine pit Rhys and I played in when we were kids."

The three men hastily exited the building, running toward the parking lot.

"We'll take my car," George called out. Milly and Garrett were with the trooper and Len, who was now sitting up with his head between his knees, a handkerchief pressed against his forehead.

"I think he'll be okay," Milly told them. "Rhys hit him with the butt of his handgun."

George spoke briefly to the trooper. "Call an ambulance to check out Mr. Paynter, then contact headquarters to have two units stand by. I'll be in touch soon to establish a rendezvous point."

Mal jumped into the passenger side as Evan yanked open a back door of the car.

"When you start down the lane toward the highway, drive fairly slowly," Mal said to George. "I think Augusta may be able to give us some signals."

"How could she do that?"

"White makeup stick. She drew an arrow on her dressing table with it. I have no idea how she managed to do that without Rhys noticing, but I'm sure she'll use it again if she has a chance."

Sure enough, as they eased toward Route 390, a tree showed a white line. And then another. And beyond that, they noted a wooded area with some broken branches.

"He had the second car stashed here," George said.

As he sped off in pursuit, they were all keenly aware Rhys had a head start on them—at least fifteen minutes.

***

Augusta had changed into her costume for the final scene and was refreshing her makeup when the door to her dressing room was flung open. She stared at Rhys as he stepped inside.

It took a moment for her to process that he had a gun pointed directly at her. He was gripping it much the same way he had gripped her wrist earlier, and she felt a strong chill run up her spine. Augusta's eyes moved to Rhys's face—his taut jaw, pinched mouth, and darting eyes told her he was deadly serious and considerably on edge.

"Not a sound," Rhys hissed.

She'd had a gun pointed at her before, but not by a man whose mental state was so frighteningly tenuous. *Breathe, Augusta. He won't shoot you here.*

Heart pounding in her ears, Augusta forced herself to remain calm. Her hand closed around the white makeup stick. "What are you doing, Rhys?" She fought to keep her voice low and even.

"You know that little talk we had earlier today? I'm going to show you something. We can talk while we're driving." He waggled the gun at her. "Get up. We're leaving."

"You know I'll be missed when I'm not onstage for this final scene." She worked the top off the makeup stick slowly as she talked, gesturing with her right hand to keep Rhys's attention away from her left hand. "I promise I'll go with you." Augusta reached out toward him. "Let me finish the show, and no one will suspect anything is wrong."

"Too late. They already suspect." He waved the gun again.

Augusta brushed a small jar off the dressing table as she turned, distracting Rhys long enough to quickly draw a line and an arrow on the table. "Oh, dear, so sorry," she murmured as he deftly caught the jar before it hit the floor. She kept the makeup stick firmly in her left hand as Rhys grabbed her right wrist with his left hand, keeping the gun in his right hand trained on her.

He stared at her for a moment, snatched her wig off, threw it under the chair, and dragged her quickly to the backstage emergency exit. The entire cast was onstage, and no one was standing near the stage right entrance door as the attention of all members of the stage crew were focused on the final scene.

Rhys pulled Augusta through the emergency door and began to move away from the building. He yanked hard on her hand, causing her to stumble.

"Pick up your damn feet."

"I'm trying. These shoes are too small." Anything to try to stall him.

"Keep moving," he barked as they moved further away from the Playhouse.

He didn't go toward the parking lot. *Now what?* "Where are we going? Don't you need your car?"

"Shut up." *Another car parked close by. Probably concealed,* she guessed.

They moved past a tree close enough for her to mark it quickly with a streak of white. Intent on getting to the vehicle, Rhys focused on dragging her along behind him, half turning to keep Augusta aware of the gun he still pointed at her.

Another tree close enough to mark. Augusta saw the car, concealed by branches in a stand of trees on the side of the lane. Rhys shoved the branches aside and pushed her into the driver's seat.

Still clutching the makeup stick, Augusta managed to stuff it into a pocket in her costume as she got into the car. "Where are we going?"

"I told you to shut up." Rhys moved around the front of the car, the gun trained on her at all times, opened the passenger door and slid inside. With his free hand he reached into his pocket and handed her the keys to the car.

"I'm not sure I can drive this car. I'm not a very good driver."

A bark of laughter. "I heard about your driving feat from the other day. Sometimes showing off is a stupid thing to do, Augusta," he sneered.

"Get out to Route 390 and turn left," Rhys ordered. "Fast enough, but not too fast. The state police will be looking for my car, not this rental. But we're still going to take back roads."

"We're going to Carbondale?"

"You'll see."

Route 191 would be the more direct route, but he wants to avoid that, Augusta thought.

"Very clever of you to conceal a second car, Rhys. How did you get back to Skytop after you hid this one?" *Keep him talking.*

"You think you're so damned smart. Guess."

"Hitchhiked? That was taking a chance. Someone might have recognized you."

"Not me. They'd have recognized Evan. He's the famous one, remember?"

Jealousy can be a powerful motivator. "You know, Rhys, Evan told us you have a beautiful voice. It could have been you with the career he's been enjoying, if you'd really wanted that."

"Just shut up."

She drove silently as they entered Promised Land State Park.

"Turn left here." A road which quickly turned to gravel. *A service road. Good, this will slow us down,* Augusta thought.

They soon left the park, and Rhys continued to issue directions which confirmed Augusta's suspicion they were going to Carbondale.

Through the fear she fought to keep from overwhelming her, Augusta felt a glimmer of hope. *Evan may have an idea where he's taking me, and it's going to take us longer to get there. They could be there when we arrive.*

Rhys was a disturbed man on some kind of a mission—Augusta was sure that her life was very much in danger. He watched her as much as he watched the road. There was very little traffic on these back roads.

What if I just crash the car? Pretend to be having some kind of trouble with it? Augusta was aware of Rhys staring at her intently. She clutched the steering wheel hard to keep her hands from shaking. *Don't let him see how frightened you are.* She caught a sharp breath and clenched her jaw.

"I don't want to kill you, Augusta," Rhys said abruptly.

The unspoken words *But I will if I have to* hung in the air.

Still, this pronouncement stunned her. "Why am I here, Rhys?" Augusta's voice quivered.

"You're my witness."

Augusta clutched the steering wheel hard. *Dear God in heaven. Is he suicidal? Entirely possible. He's also deeply disturbed and all of this could change in an instant.*

***

Consulting a map, Evan pointed out the exact location of the abandoned mine to George, and the two of them quickly agreed on the best location for their meet-up with the other state troopers. As they drove up Route 191, heading directly toward Carbondale, George contacted the Pennsylvania State Police barracks in Mt. Pocono to request the rendezvous.

He had an additional request for other units and local police departments to be on the lookout for Rhys.

"Rental car, one driver, one passenger. One white male, one white female, both with dark hair. Both mid-forties. Female may be the driver."

"Why do you think Augusta may be driving?" Evan asked.

"It's likely Rhys is holding his weapon on her and would be unable to drive," Malcolm explained to Evan.

"I understand. You're alerting the local police as well?"

"You never know what you might find if you spread a wide enough net," George told him. "Or how Augusta might react if she sees a police car approaching them." He glanced at Mal, who nodded.

"She's a very savvy lady and might find some way to signal a patrol car," Mal said. "How long until we reach Carbondale?"

"About another forty minutes," George replied. "But Rhys will most likely not use a direct route, so there's only a slim chance of Augusta seeing a cop on her drive."

"I don't believe Rhys is thinking straight at all," Evan said.

"If he's figured an alternate route in order to avoid the PSP, he's thinking straighter than we'd like him to be," George said, grimly. "There are a lot of roads he could use to end up at Salem Mountain. Our advantage could be we might get to that location before he does."

Malcolm stared ahead into the darkness as they rode in silence for a few miles. *Keep your wits about you, Augusta.* Without thinking, he began praying silently to St. Michael the Archangel, patron saint of all law enforcement officers. *St. Michael the Archangel, defend us in battle. Be our protection against the malice and snares of the devil. May God rebuke him, we humbly pray…please keep her safe.*

George adjusted his rear-view mirror. "Why would he abduct Augusta? That's one thing I can't figure out. He only met her recently, and they haven't spent much time together."

"Sorry to say, Augusta went to see him this afternoon," Mal told them. He let out a deep breath. "It seemed harmless enough and she spent only a few minutes with him, but for someone as volatile and confused as Rhys is, it likely triggered this whole episode."

George glanced in Evan's direction. "You aren't aware of this. We've learned Joan Cromer's mother found a letter Rhys wrote to Joan which indicates she dumped him because he didn't compare favorably to you."

The men didn't speak for a few minutes, each lost in his own thoughts.

"This isn't about Augusta. It's about what's between Rhys and me," Evan said slowly. "I believe Rhys knew if he abducted Augusta, I'd come after him. And I would know exactly where he would take her. He's looking for—some kind of a showdown. Retribution."

Malcolm stared out of the window into the darkness, fighting a growing sense of fear and frustration.

Chapter 17
A Tragic Life

Augusta drove the rental car deeper into the countryside, Rhys still training the gun on her.

What do you want with me, Rhys? "*I don't want to kill you, Augusta*"—"*You're my witness.*" A sudden realization. *Rhys knew Evan would come after me. This is about the two of them. Something—unresolved. Joan, maybe? Maybe more. Maybe a lot more. Is there any way I can get him to start talking? Not as long as he's pointing that gun at me.*

Gradually, Rhys seemed to relax slightly. He laid the gun on his knee, his fingers still on the grip but not the trigger.

Augusta, acutely aware of him studying her closely, wasn't sure what that meant. *Don't drop your guard, Augusta.*

Long moments passed in silence. They encountered few other vehicles along this remote stretch of country road. Augusta sought frantically to think of a way to open a conversation, but surprisingly, Rhys spoke first.

"We'd have called you 'Little Miss Rich Bitch,'" he said abruptly, sounding petulant. "I mean, your family had plenty of money, you lived in a nice house in Philadelphia. Maybe you even had a couple of servants. You came to the Poconos every summer and lived in a community of wealthy people."

"Yes, that's all true."

"Your kind can't even imagine how different my life was back then—no matter how much Evan may have told you. Growing up in a mining community does things to you. Things you have no idea about."

Talking about his childhood, this is good. He sounds fairly rational at the moment. "I know the mining companies owned most of the homes. And miners sometimes had to buy everything from the company store using scrip. My understanding is that it was nearly impossible for families to save money or to buy a car."

"What do you know about Carbondale? Do you know why the town is even there?"

"That I do know. Because of the anthracite coal discovered there in the early part of the nineteenth century. No, actually, if I remember correctly, anthracite coal was discovered in Pennsylvania even earlier than that. Before 1800, I think."

"Where'd you learn that? Not from your fancy-schmantzy private school in Philadelphia," he sneered. "Or the Conservatory of Music in Cincinnati."

"My uncle."

"That's right. The conservationist who wants to reclaim the ruined land. Good luck with that." Rhys's gaze shifted as he talked. "Carbondale was intended to be the hub of the Industrial Revolution in the United States. All that coal for fuel, and then the railroads that had to be available to move the coal throughout the northeast. Carbondale had the coal, and then the railroads. Yet the hopes of the city fathers were never realized." A sigh, and he stared ahead. "Carbondale is dying. Everything is dying."

Augusta tensed, glancing at the gun. Rhys remained quiet for a few minutes, staring at the landscape moving by.

"Do you think you could live out here?" he suddenly blurted out. "Be a farm girl?" He snickered. "No, I guess not. You're a city girl. You come from privilege. What's that like, anyway?"

Does he really want an answer? Before she could reply, Rhys started talking rapidly again. "Miners beget miners. I was expected to follow in my father's footsteps. Just as Evan was. You knew our dads were twins, didn't you? It was more than that. Both of them sired only one child. Evan and I were more than cousins. We were like brothers."

He paused, as if expecting a comment, and Augusta responded. "I didn't know that, Rhys. It makes what you did for him all the more admirable—teaching Evan to protect himself from bullies. And even more, encouraging him when he wanted to be a singer."

"My father hated that I did that...even when it looked like Evan might end up a famous singer. My father resented it, you know? Resented that Evan was going to be successful. But he never told me he was sorry he didn't let me try."

Now he once again sounds more like a petulant child than a man in his forties. "That's very sad."

They approached an intersection and Rhys's hand tightened on the gun and his eyes darted to the left and to the right. "Slow down...now stop."

Augusta eased to a stop, her heart pounding. *We must be getting close to the mine.*

Not seeing any traffic, he motioned for her to drive across the highway and continue along the back road they'd been traveling. The narrow road began to climb and wind.

Rhys resumed talking. "Evan's time in the Army was one of the best things that ever happened to him...." He paused. "I was in the Marines, you know. I did two tours."

"In Europe?" *That's good, keep him talking.*

"The first tour there, the other in the South Pacific near the end of the war. Whatever that was worth...." Another pause, then almost to himself, "I needed to find some way to be somebody. I mean, after I came home. To be famous. Famous like Evan was. I thought maybe I found a way for a while there."

"The Conowingo Project," Augusta guessed.

"The best time of my life," he responded. "Met some brilliant guys. This might surprise you, but they really liked me. They appreciated what I could do. That project could have resurrected Carbondale. I'd have finally made my dad proud of me. Then it was shut down." His voice dropped to a monotone as he pointed the gun straight ahead. "My life hasn't been the same since. Nothing's been the same since. The mines started to die."

Rhys stared into space for a time. Augusta glanced at him. His eyes seemed dead. "Then the Knox disaster happened. Probably the end of anthracite mining here. Lives lost, and for what? My father gone forever. The end of dreams."

What dreams? Augusta wondered. "Yet you were working on a way to resurrect the Conowingo Project."

"I despise mining and everything about it," Rhys said vehemently. "Have you ever been inside a mine, Augusta?"

"No, I have not." *He's all over the place. How far will he go with this?*

"Let me introduce you to our noble profession." His voice dripped with sarcasm. "Once you get past the entrance and are deep inside the mine, there is no light…absolutely none. It's a blackness unlike any other. Without their lighted helmets and torches, miners would be totally unable to function. Without light, you start to lose all sense of direction. The ceiling in the room can be so low that you can't even stand erect." He slouched down in his seat, as if he were experiencing it as he spoke. "And the water. The constant dripping of water."

Augusta shuddered. "It sounds dreadful." She thought of her experience of being in utter darkness once in her life not too many months earlier. Another abduction, when she had been drugged and awoke in a basement in complete darkness. *But there was a sliver of light there*, she recalled. *And I had the light on my wristwatch.* Still, it had been frightening.

"Miners pretend they get used to it. They see themselves as some kind of warrior. It's one of the most difficult jobs a man can have. You never really know when you go to work if you're going to come out alive. Every morning you go into the mine, sometimes before the sun comes up, and you leave the mine sometimes when it's already dark. All that darkness starts to seep into a man's soul. It changes you. It changes the way you look at life."

Rhys lifted the gun at an angle, staring at the barrel, as he slowly put his finger on the trigger. Augusta gripped the wheel harder. *Good Lord. Is he going to shoot?*

Rhys straightened, took his finger off the trigger and said, matter-of-factly, "It will be an excellent thing when mining in the Anthracite Region completely dies."

Once her racing heart slowed, Augusta asked, "But what about the Conowingo Project? And your renewed work on it? Weren't you hoping to revive anthracite mining?"

"That was a ruse," Rhys said scornfully. "I was hoping to bankrupt the Big Plains Mining Company."

Augusta was taken aback by this and drove silently for a few minutes. "How could you have done that, Rhys? I don't think anyone had any idea."

"I had a plan," Rhys sneered. "I had a budget all ready for them. More money than they could have afforded, but it was a workable budget. I'm a smart person. And I'd have spent it, and would have needed

230

more, and more. I'd have hired people. Bought supplies. And then disappeared."

His tone of voice changed as he nodded his head. "I did tell one person."

Careful, Augusta. Don't say anything.

"I told Joan."

Be very careful how you respond. After a moment she said, "Joan Cromer?"

"Yes, Joan Cromer. Don't sound so surprised. I'm sure you were aware I knew her."

"How would I have known that?" Augusta gripped the wheel tighter, feeling the tension shoot up her spine and across her shoulders.

"Come on, Augusta. Joan was from Cincinnati. The police would have interviewed her parents. Maybe your detective interviewed them. I'm not a complete idiot."

"Yes, Malcolm did talk to them, but I don't believe your name was ever mentioned."

Rhys gripped the gun more tightly. "Right. I figured that out when I didn't hear from the state police after Joan was found in the Playhouse parking lot," he said loudly, waving the gun. "She must never have told her parents about us."

Think fast, Augusta. "From what I understand, she didn't tell her parents much about her life."

"She told them about Evan, though. All about wonderful Evan." His voice dripped bitter sarcasm.

Rhys turned toward Augusta and spoke slowly, almost in a whisper. "I really loved Joan. We had something special. We could have been...they think I killed her, you know? Do you think I killed her?" Rhys sounded anything but rational. "Why would I have killed her? I loved her. More than I'd ever loved anybody." He pointed the gun at Augusta's head. "Do you think I killed her?"

Augusta nearly stopped breathing as her hands froze to the steering wheel. She could barely choke out words past the knot in her throat. "Why would I think that, Rhys?'

"Well, I was there…that night…I saw her in the parking lot…then I looked down and she was on the ground…she looked like she was dead.…"

He went silent for a moment, then resumed speaking, rapidly. "You know about our childhood, don't you? Mine and Evan's?" Rhys didn't wait for her to respond, but began tapping the gun barrel on the side of the steering wheel. "I taught him how to fight. How to defend himself. I told everybody they should let him sing." He paused again.

Augusta jumped in, hoping to keep his thoughts on happier times. "Evan knows all that. He told me himself how much he owes you for the life he's enjoying now."

"I was happy for him." Rhys spoke even faster, his voice rising slightly in pitch. It reminded Augusta of his frenzied pontification at brunch on Monday, words spilling over each other. "When he got out of the service I went to Philadelphia and heard him sing in an opera at Temple University. He was the best performer on that stage. Then he got a scholarship at Indiana University and kept singing. People at home didn't appreciate what he was doing for a long time. You know when they finally stopped thinking of him as some kind of freak?

When the movie *The Great Caruso* came out. When Mario Lanza, the kid from Philadelphia, became famous. Then some people at home started saying maybe Evan was going to be famous like Lanza was. Evan paid for our family to stay at a nice hotel in New York when he made his Metropolitan Opera debut, did you know that? He paid for the trip. He was proud to have us there. I was so proud of him. I really loved my cousin."

Another pause, then more disjointed thoughts spewed out. "I'd been trying to find some way to turn my life around. Things went all to hell for me when the Conowingo Tunnel Project fell apart. Then my dad was lost in the Knox Mine disaster. I left home and went out west. I couldn't figure out who I was anymore. I didn't know what to do. I hated mining but I didn't seem to be able to break away from it."

The tone of his voice grew warmer. "Then the most incredible thing happened. I met Joan at a conference in Cincinnati. When we first met, she came up to me from behind and tapped me on the shoulder. I turned and looked at her. For me, it was love at first sight. We had an amazing weekend together. I made arrangements for us to meet in Pittsburgh a couple of weeks later. It was even better than our first weekend. I wanted to marry Joan. She made me feel good about myself. I started to think maybe I could have a decent life if I had Joan."

Augusta's eyes ached and burned. Every muscle in her body throbbed from the effort of driving. Rhys's mood swings and erratic ramblings were frightening. *He could go off the deep end at any moment, and then what do I do?*

A longer pause, and when he resumed Rhys spoke more slowly, his words taking on an increasing bitterness. "We got together one final time. We met in Cleveland. That's when Joan finally told me about Evan. She claimed she couldn't marry me because Evan wanted her. Some of the things she said didn't make any sense. I realized her relationship with Evan wasn't real. She was obsessed with him."

A sharp bark of laughter. "Oh, this you'll appreciate." Rhys leaned forward, resting his right arm on the dashboard, staring at Augusta, still clutching the gun. "When we were in Cleveland, she told me the only reason she was with me was because she had at first mistaken me for Evan. She had spent time with me because she could pretend I was my cousin." A deep breath. "And the hell of it is, I was okay with that. I still wanted her. I could accept that. But she insisted it was over."

And that's why you killed her. She rejected you. You weren't Evan.

He straightened to see where they were. "Turn left here. Drive slowly, this is only a trail into the woods. Turn on the high beams."

Augusta needed all her driving skills for this. She slowed considerably as the road—what there was of it—turned sharply downhill and as Rhys had cautioned, narrowed to nothing more than a trail. Branches brushed the top and sides of the car more than once and she drove over some large rocks, holding her breath as she waited to hear a tire pop. *Where in the world are we?*

"Stop here," he barked out. "We walk the rest of the way."

***

The drive to Carbondale was the longest forty minutes of Malcolm Mitchell's life. Every moment of the time he'd had with Augusta ran through his mind, from their first acrimonious encounter to the final words he had spoken to her before they left Lenny's house that evening. He clung to the hope Evan had offered when he declared Rhys was using Augusta as bait to draw them to this upcoming confrontation between the cousins.

"It's a mine that was abandoned decades ago," Evan told them. "The first one the Big Plains Mining Company ever dug here. The beginning of the destruction of the land. Once a mine had all the ore that could possibly be removed dug out, the company just walked away from it. They didn't even close the opening. Anybody could go into it and do whatever they wanted. No warning signs about how unstable and dangerous those abandoned mines are. The breaker was left to rot and crumble. And of course, no thought was ever given to reclaiming the land that had been ruined."

George asked Evan, "You think we might get there before Rhys does?"

"I think it's a definite possibility. But we need to approach with caution in case I'm wrong. I think the three of us should stick together. Trooper LaBar, I'd suggest you deploy your men on each side and we'll approach from the front. Only let me go first. Maybe Mal and me. There are plenty of places around the mine opening to stay concealed. The breaker, slag heaps. Trees and bushes. And the fact that it's dark works in our favor."

"We all have strong flashlights."

"We'll need them," Evan said grimly.

"You played there when you were a kid?" Mal asked, incredulously.

"Sure did. We all did, all of us miners' kids. Swam in those filthy pools. Watch out for those, they're deeper than they look. Stay away from them."

George LaBar drove up a road on the east side of Carbondale and now eased his patrol car to a stop. Evan had told George the mine was about a mile and a half hike from that spot...their rendezvous point...and he'd relayed the information to the troopers who were to meet them.

"All right, Evan. We have two cars meeting us in the next few minutes," George said. "What's the best way to get to the mine?" He handed Evan a pen and pad. "Can you draw a rough sketch of what's there?"

Evan sketched quickly as he described the area. "There's an old road up the backside of the mountain which nobody ever uses anymore, but it's still visible. My guess is Rhys will have Augusta drive up that way, park in the woods, and climb down to the mine. I know exactly where he would park. Let me check that before we do anything else. If his car isn't there yet, we have the advantage."

He continued, "Here's the opening to Big Plains Number One. Here's what little is left of the breaker. It's

been falling apart for decades. Slag heaps here and here."
He made Xs, then drew a circle to the side of one of the
Xs. "The pond. Easy to step into it if you aren't careful."

Within minutes, both state cars pulled up beside
them.

"Okay, Evan. This is as far as you go," George said
firmly.

"What are you talking about? It's me Rhys wants.
He has to see me."

"You're a civilian. I can't put you in the line of fire."
George nodded toward Malcolm. "I probably shouldn't
involve Malcolm in this either, but I'm making an
exception. This isn't his jurisdiction. But Augusta is his
wife, and he's a cop."

Evan became increasingly agitated. "Rhys isn't in
his right mind. We all know that. If he doesn't get what
he wants—which is to confront me—he's capable of
killing Augusta. And I think he's suicidal. You could
have two dead people in the first two minutes you
confront him."

Mal spoke up. "I know it's highly unusual, George,
but I think you have to make another exception for
Evan—I believe his assessment is correct."

"I don't like it," George snapped. He walked away
from them for a moment, staring off into the darkness.
He turned back to them. "There will probably be hell to
pay, but okay, we'll do it your way, Evan."

Guns drawn, Malcolm and George flanked Evan as
they hiked toward the mine, using only the dim light of
the waning crescent moon.

Words Evan had spoken earlier echoed in Malcolm's head:

This isn't going to end well.

Chapter 18
Big Plains Number One

"Why are you so sure Evan will follow us?"

Rhys was behind Augusta, still holding the gun but also shining a flashlight ahead of her so she could see where to step.

"This mine has special significance for us. We used to play here. When he was thirteen and I was fifteen, I saved his life here when he was attacked by three bullies. Then four years later we fought four S.O.B.s and did a real number on them."

She found it unfathomable that kids had played in such a place. That their families had permitted it. Everything about this was beyond her comprehension.

Rhys waved the flashlight in circles, causing Augusta to stumble. "That was the day I told Evan he'd become a man. We made a vow if either of us ever needed the other, we'd meet here—at Big Plains Number One."

He mentioned that mine at brunch, Augusta thought. She clutched at a bush, feeling sharp pricks on her palm, as the descent became steeper. "That was nearly thirty years ago. Do you think he'd remember that conversation?"

"Yeah, he'll remember. And I have the one thing he wanted he never got. You."

That's nonsense, Augusta thought. "He has me. We've become close friends."

"You know damn well what I mean. It's not the same. He'll come."

A sudden chill as she stumbled a second time. *Dear Lord, does he plan to shoot me in front of Evan? No, I can't believe that. He says he's using me for bait.*

Augusta stopped and stared in dismay at the next part of the path they were following. "Rhys, there is no way I can climb down that in a long skirt."

"Then take the damned thing off," he barked impatiently.

Instead, Augusta recalled climbing a rock wall the day she met Malcolm. She reached behind her, gathered up the back part of the skirt, gathered the front part, and tied the two together at the front.

"Very resourceful. You've done this before."

"In a way, yes."

Rhys was speaking in a nearly normal tone. *Could I possibly try to reason with him? Probably not. I've seen how lightning quick his mood swings can be.*

Now all Augusta's attention was focused on making the final descent, as she frantically grabbed at bushes and rocks to keep her balance. One sleeve ripped halfway up her arm. She felt a rock scrape her left leg but ignored the pain and the blood she felt trickling down her shin. *Let's just get this over with.*

They reached the bottom of the incline and Augusta caught her breath as she shook out her dress. Rhys shone the flashlight around the area. Augusta could make out the partially collapsed wooden breaker and two culm heaps. *How old is this mine?*

Rhys directed the light to the entrance of the mine…and Augusta stopped breathing.

What she saw appeared to her as the stuff nightmares are made of. The only light came from Rhys's flashlight and the waning moon. She heard no sounds at all—only absolute stillness. Railroad tracks approached the opening, which Augusta perceived as a wound in the side of the mountain. Beyond was total blackness.

A wave of intense dread spread over her and she felt her throat close. *What horrors has this place been witness to?*

She stared for long moments at the portal and the sense of dread increased.

"I can't go in there. I cannot." Her voice cracked.

"Keep moving," he snapped.

She turned and faced him, "I mean it, Rhys. There is no way I can walk into that mine."

The tension between them heightened over what seemed a long moment of silence. Augusta closed her eyes, wondering if he might actually shoot her.

"Let her go, Rhys."

Evan's voice. He stepped outside the mine entrance holding a strong flashlight pointed upward, lighting his face. "This isn't about Augusta. It's between you and me."

Augusta shivered violently and almost wept with relief. *Malcolm must be here.*

Rhys dropped his flashlight, grabbed Augusta's arm and yanked her in front of him, the gun pointed at her head. She froze, plunged again into fear.

"Yes, between you and me," Rhys hissed, pressing the gun more firmly against Augusta's temple.

Dear God, I've been in this situation once before. But the man holding the gun then wasn't mentally unbalanced. Rhys could pull the trigger and not even know what he was doing. She tried hard to control her breathing.

"Evan Llewellyn, the man who has everything," Rhys sneered. "And Rhys Llewellyn, the man who has nothing." He laughed bitterly.

Evan stared at Rhys and Augusta, his eyes moving from one to the other. He chose his words carefully. "I regret...all the difficulties that you've had in your life, Rhys." A pause. "I wish I had reached out to you more. Maybe I could have been of some help. The way you helped me when I was a kid."

More laughter from Rhys. "What could you have done, Evan? Life happens." His voice rose shrilly. "For you, it was good. For me...it could hardly have been worse."

Augusta became aware of two shadows moving forward to stand on either side of Evan. *Malcolm. And George LaBar.*

"Maybe we'd have found a way to get you away from the mines," Evan said.

Two flashlights from either side of Evan revealed Mal and George, each with a gun leveled at Rhys.

Augusta saw Mal struggling to contain his emotions. She caught his eyes and held them, drawing strength from knowing he was there.

"How would you have accomplished that, Evan? Made me part of your act somehow? Your manager?" He spat out the words, pressing the gun harder against Augusta's temple, and she closed her eyes in pain.

Malcolm took a step closer. "Let Augusta go, Rhys. We can talk this out."

"Can we? I don't think so. This is it, isn't it, Evan?" More shrill laughter. "*The end game.* Isn't that what it's called? Like chess."

"Malcolm is right, Rhys. Let Augusta go. She's not part of this." Evan shone his flashlight directly into Rhys's face.

"Look, no one has been harmed to this point, Llewellyn," George said, edging forward. "Let's go back to Mt. Pocono and talk. I'm sure you have things you'd like us to know. But first, you have to release Mrs. Mitchell. I know you don't want to hurt her."

"Don't I?" Rhys's eyes darted from Malcolm to George. "I sure as hell want to hurt *somebody*!" he suddenly screamed.

Rhys had tightened his hold on Augusta, and she clawed at his arm, feeling her breath being cut off. Rhys seemed to realize he was on the verge of choking her and relaxed his grip a bit. Augusta gasped for air.

With no warning, Rhys abruptly shoved Augusta in Malcolm's direction. Augusta stumbled, her legs giving way, as Malcolm sprang forward and caught her in his free arm before she fell.

Rhys quickly turned the gun toward his temple. *"This is what I want."* His shouted words echoed from the mine entrance.

Frozen, they all heard the sound of the hammer being cocked.

"NO!" Evan cried out, taking a step toward his cousin. "Don't do it, Rhys. Talk to me. Tell me what I can do."

A trembling Augusta leaned against Malcolm, closing her eyes at this new development. *That's what he meant when he said I was to be his witness. He wanted someone to know why he intends to kill himself. If Evan hadn't been here when we arrived....*

"You had everything. I had nothing. *You stole the life I should have had.* I could deal with it all, until Joan. Until you stole my one chance at happiness." A sob deep in his throat. "Do you know how it felt last Christmas, listening to you talk about how Joan was stalking you...*stalking* you?"

"Why didn't you tell me about her then?" Evan implored. "I could have talked to her. You deserved her love so much more than I did."

"Talked to her? *Talked to her?*" More shrill laughter. "What would you have said to her? It wouldn't have done any good."

"When did you last see Miss Cromer?" LaBar had a case to solve. "We know about the last letter you wrote her. Her mother found it in a drawer."

Rhys's eyes darted wildly from one man to the next. "I saw her the afternoon of the opening night of *Carousel*. She told me again that we were through, and when she left, I knew she would go to Evan. I couldn't stop thinking about it. So, on Wednesday night I went to the Playhouse. I found her in the parking lot...we talked...the next thing I remember is seeing her lying on the ground. It seemed like she was dead."

His eyes fixed on Evan. "She was obsessed with you. But I could have made her happy. I would have given her anything she wanted."

Augusta became acutely aware of the way George was staring at Rhys. *He wants to try to knock the gun away*, she thought. She had seen Malcolm do exactly that when she was being held at gunpoint. He had leaped forward and knocked the gunman's hand upward. But he'd had a distraction, a moment when the gunman relaxed his guard.

"I could have talked to her," Evan repeated, frantic with fear.

"She never loved me," Rhys said flatly. "My life is over."

Abruptly, Augusta spoke up, "That's not true. She kept your letter. She had feelings for you. If she hadn't, she would have thrown the letter away." She knew it was a long shot, but it was the best she could come up with.

It was enough. George saw his moment and took it, leaping forward, thrusting both arms under Rhys's and getting his hand around the hand holding the gun. The two men swayed as they struggled for control. George prevailed, and when Rhys pulled the trigger, the gun discharged into the mine entrance as George stripped the gun from Rhys's hand.

Two things happened simultaneously. On hearing the gunshot, four state troopers burst on the scene, guns drawn, strong flashlights illuminating the area. And from the mine, a blinding flash of light followed immediately by the intense percussive sound of an explosion, so strong Augusta felt it in her chest.

She was aware of shouts and the sound of men running. Malcolm lifted her into his arms and swiftly moved both of them farther away from the mine entrance. A dense cloud of black smoke rolled from the portal, enveloping all of them. Augusta heard coughing and pressed her face against Malcolm's chest, struggling to breathe.

A rumbling sound began to grow and in moments became an ominous roar. Chunks of earth and rock rained down on them. More running and shouting in the chaos and confusion.

Malcolm hurriedly lowered Augusta to the ground and covered her body with his to protect her from the falling debris.

The roar gradually began to subside and the deluge of debris slowed and ceased. Hacking and coughing, the troopers brushed away earth and rocks from those lying on the ground. The smoke thinned.

"What the hell just happened?"..."Some kind of explosion."..."There must have been old explosives stored near the entrance."..."What happened to the mine?"

All flashlights were turned toward the mine entrance. They stared silently.

It was no more. Big Plains Number One was gone, the entrance collapsed into a steaming pile of rubble. Clouds of smoke drifted upward from the dead mine.

Mal assisted Augusta to a sitting position and then helped her to her feet. "Are you all right?"

Struggling to breathe, she managed to gasp, "I will be...what just happened?"

"My guess is the bullet hit some old explosives and set them off." He wiped her face gently with his handkerchief, removing soot left from the cloud of smoke. "Are you sure you aren't hurt?"

"I don't think so. What about you?"

"I'm fine."

A short distance away Evan worked frantically to clear dirt and debris from a prone Rhys, lying motionless on the ground. One of the troopers helped him pull Rhys to a sitting position and pound on his back. Augusta wasn't sure he was breathing until he began coughing violently. Evan knelt beside him, taking Rhys in his arms and rocking him.

Rhys leaned back and stared at his cousin. "Evan?"

"Thank God you're all right." Evan was in tears.

"Evan? What happened?" Rhys glanced around, dazed. "Why are we here?"

He struggled to his feet, and immediately George LaBar put an unresisting Rhys in handcuffs. "Rhys Llewellyn, I am placing you under arrest for the kidnapping and assault of Augusta McKee Mitchell."

Rhys looked at Evan again. "Evan?" He seemed not to comprehend what was happening.

Evan put both hands on his cousin's shoulders. His voice shook as he spoke. "I'll get you the best lawyer we can find, Rhys. You didn't mean to do any of this."

"Move away from the prisoner, Mr. Llewellyn," George ordered forcefully.

Evan took a step back but stayed close, continuing to talk. "You're not well. Don't say anything until I bring your lawyer to you."

Rhys made no response, not even looking at Evan. George handed him off to two of the troopers to be taken to Monroe County.

"Do you have to put him in jail?" Evan pleaded. "He needs to be under a doctor's care. You can see he's...he doesn't even know what's happening."

"For tonight we don't have any other choice," George responded. "We'll keep him under suicide watch."

Evan ran a hand over the back of his neck. "You didn't charge him with Joan's murder."

"We still have to learn what actually happened. He confessed to being there. We all heard him claim he doesn't remember anything about the murder."

"I believe him."

George turned to the other two troopers. "Stay here for the present. I'm sure there may be people who heard the explosion. One of you contact the Carbondale police and assist them if they request it."

They nodded, and one went back to the car to contact the local police.

George put a hand on Evan's shoulder and nodded to Mal and Augusta. "You three come with me."

The four of them walked slowly back to George's car, all of them attempting to absorb what had just taken place. Mal put an arm around Augusta's waist. "Stop for a minute, please. I need to see why Augusta's limping."

Lifting the long skirt revealed an ugly scratch that oozed blood. "That must have happened when I climbed down the hill," Augusta said as Mal pressed his handkerchief to the wound.

"It needs to be looked at," he said to George. "Where can we take her?"

Evan spoke up. "Take her to my parents' house. My mom is a great nurse. She can perform first aid until we get to a hospital."

"I don't need a hospital. I'm sure it will be fine," Augusta said. Her voice broke. "I just want to go home and go to bed." A sharp intake of breath, almost a sob. "Lenny will have first aid supplies. Please, I just want to go home."

George had been examining Augusta's leg. "First aid kit in my patrol car. We can fix it up for the present, but you should have it looked at tomorrow, Augusta."

They reached the car and George produced the first aid kit, handing it to Malcolm. With a movement of his head, George indicated to Evan that they should move away and leave Mal and Augusta alone.

Augusta sat sideways in the front passenger seat, her legs outside the car, and watched as Mal knelt and gently cleaned and dressed her wound. "It should heal fine. It's not deep."

She leaned her head against his shoulder, and as a wave of realization swept over her, she began to sob. "Rhys was out of his mind...and his gun...and that explosion. We could all have been killed. And I was so frightened that you wouldn't find me in time." The wrenching sobs shook her entire body. "Mal, I'm so sorry."

Mal held her and rocked her until she grew quieter. "None of this was your fault, Gus. You don't have anything to be sorry about. You kept your head and most likely saved Rhys's life."

"For what? We all know he killed Joan. He's probably going to jail for the rest of his life. But he's sick, Mal. He's desperately ill."

"Yes, I agree. There's a lot to be sorted out." He gently kissed her forehead. "But for now, you're safe and in my arms, and this night is over."

He held her close as they drove back to Monroe County in silence, lost in their own thoughts.

Chapter 19
Aftermath

Thursday, June 16, 3:00 a.m.

As the car entered Buck Hill, Evan turned toward George LaBar.

"Where will they take him? Can I be with him?" His voice shook. "You saw how he was. He doesn't even know what's happening to him."

"Rhys is at the PSP barracks in Mt. Pocono," George replied. "No, you won't be able to see him tonight. They'll process him—take his picture and fingerprints— and prepare the charges. After that he'll be taken to the Monroe County jail in Stroudsburg. The officers there will take good care of him, Evan. He'll be safe."

"I'm going to ask Garrett to represent him. Shouldn't he be there while this is happening?"

"Not necessary," George replied. "Tomorrow Rhys will be formally arraigned at the District Magistrate's Office in Mountainhome, and Garrett needs to be present for that. I'll call Garrett first thing in the morning. He may want to request a preliminary psychiatric evaluation as soon as possible after the arraignment."

"What would be the purpose of that?" Evan ran a hand over the back of his neck.

"There are serious charges against Rhys," George said. "The judge won't even consider releasing him on bail, he'd be confined. But if the psych evaluation indicates his mental state precludes him being able to even understand the charges, it's possible he could be remanded to a mental hospital. There's a state facility in the Lehigh Valley, but it will be a day or two before he can be transferred from the county jail."

"I know about the charges involving Augusta, but will he be charged with Joan's murder?" Evan asked.

"It's certainly possible," George told him.

When they arrived at Len's, Mal saw Emily waiting anxiously at the bottom of the steps. She quickly pulled Evan's car door open and reached for him. Her arms wrapped around his waist, Emily led Evan into the house.

Milly and Garrett came to the car as Mal carefully helped Augusta out. Mal saw the shock on Milly's face at Augusta's ashen, slightly dazed appearance.

"Mal—" Milly stared at him in dismay.

He shook his head and mouthed *not now*. "You made sure Emily would be here, didn't you? Good call."

"I insisted she come back with us. We stopped at the cast house and she packed a few things."

George stepped out of the car. "How's Len?"

"He should be fine," Garrett responded. "The hospital wanted to keep him overnight, though, just to be on the safe side."

George turned to Mal. "Will I see you tomorrow at the arraignment?"

"Most likely, if I'm not intruding."

"Not at all. I'd like to see you there." He turned to Augusta. "You're a remarkable person, Mrs. Mitchell. I'm honored to know you."

Augusta took a deep breath. "I'm sorry I fell apart." Mal tightened his arm around her waist.

"I didn't see that. I saw a lady who kept her cool when lives depended on it and had a natural reaction at the end of a harrowing ordeal."

"I knew I liked you, Trooper LaBar." Augusta managed a smile of gratitude.

George returned the smile and saluted her before pulling away.

Back in the house, Milly poured brandy for all of them as Mal briefly filled her and Garrett in on what had happened in Carbondale. He glanced occasionally at Evan sitting on the sofa, still in Emily's arms, his head on her shoulder.

"Garrett, I need you to represent Rhys." Evan pulled himself up. "No matter the cost, whatever you need. I want him to have the best."

Garrett nodded. "Of course. I assume he'll be arraigned in the morning."

"That's what George—Trooper LaBar said. Something happened to Rhys when that explosion took place." Evan ran a hand over his hair. "He doesn't seem to—well, he's not connecting with reality, is the way I see it."

"Some kind of psychotic break, maybe," Garrett commented.

Evan stood, Emily at his side. "Thank you." He glanced around the room. His voice faltered as he continued, "Please…forgive me. I need to have some time…."

"Try to get some rest," Milly said to Evan as Emily led him upstairs.

Garrett poured a second round of brandy. Augusta took a healthy swallow; it brought some color back to what had been a chalky pallor.

Milly, hands on hips, studied Malcolm and Augusta. "I want all of your clothes so I can throw them in the washer. Mal, that jacket…," she shook her head. "I'll see what I can do with it. And Augusta, that costume may be fixable, but maybe not."

"You're doing laundry at this hour?" Augusta said incredulously.

"Well, I can't sleep. I might as well do something useful."

"Don't worry about the costume. I can find something else to wear for the last three shows." Augusta took another drink of brandy. "Oh, this is good."

Milly stared at her. "You're going to perform tonight? I know you have an understudy."

"I need to. And I'm sure Evan feels the same way." Augusta stretched her leg out and grimaced. "This hurts, though." She gestured at the bandage on her shin.

Mal finished his brandy and stood. "You need a long, hot bath and a good night's sleep. Well, a good morning's sleep. Just sleep as long as you can."

Once they were upstairs, Mal began drawing a bath for Augusta.

"I can do this by myself...honestly, I'm feeling much better now," she protested.

"This was a tough night for both of us." Malcolm took a deep breath. "I was afraid I was going to lose you, Gus." His voice caught. "Won't you humor me and let me spoil you a little?"

Their eyes met. She smiled her assent and softly kissed him. Malcolm helped her undress and step into the tub. He sat on the side and bathed her tenderly. He washed her hair, toweled her dry, changed the dressing on her leg, carried her into their room, and gently laid her on the bed.

The brandy, the hot bath, and Malcolm's ministrations worked their magic. "You've made this night seem like a bad dream...with a much happier ending," Augusta murmured, her eyes closed.

"I feel better, too," he smiled. "I'll grab a quick shower and be right back."

She was drifting in and out of sleep when he returned, lay beside her, and lovingly wrapped her in his arms. Augusta's breathing became more even and steady, and Mal hoped that meant she was floating into blessed oblivion.

***

Augusta squinted at the clock on the dresser to see it was well past 11:00 a.m. The events of the night before came back to her in fragments, like the memories of a bad dream.

She focused her thoughts on Mal. Everything he had done. The way she had been confident, once she knew he was at the mine, that she wouldn't die. She sat up and examined her leg, which was less painful and looked somewhat better.

Why is it so quiet here? I don't hear anyone talking. She heard sounds from the kitchen, threw on a pair of white slacks and a daffodil-colored blouse, and made her way downstairs.

"Well, Sleeping Beauty. Good to see you," Milly commented as Augusta wandered into the kitchen just before noon. "Feeling better?"

"Yes, thanks. I smell coffee." Augusta perched at the kitchen island as Milly set a cup down in front of her.

"Good Lord, Augusta. What happened to you last night was unbelievably scary."

"It felt surreal. It still feels surreal. It's hard to believe it actually happened."

"You're dealing with it well."

"I don't know that I'm dealing with it at all yet. I keep thinking of everything Malcolm did, though. He was magnificent, Milly."

"Your hero detective. I wouldn't have expected less from him."

Augusta took a sip of coffee. "I don't know what to think about Rhys. I know Evan's worried about him. Right now, a part of me prays I never lay eyes on him again. A part of me realizes he's an incredibly disturbed person who most likely didn't realize what he was doing. That's tragic."

"Well, no doubt that's true." Milly folded her arms across her chest and leaned against the counter. "But because of Rhys you could have died."

"We all could have died. If we'd been inside the mine when that gun went off…" Augusta shuddered and took a gulp of coffee. "I pray I'm never, ever in a situation like that again."

"I'd think Malcolm must feel the same way."

Augusta set her coffee cup down and leaned forward. "He was pretty shaken, too, though of course Detective Mitchell is too much of a professional to let people see it."

Milly smiled. "Remember when you met Mal? And I referred to him as 'your detective' for the first time?"

Augusta returned the smile. "I do remember that. I told you he wasn't *my* detective and you said, 'Not yet.'"

She glanced around the room. "Speaking of Mal, where is everybody, anyway?"

"First at Rhys's preliminary hearing and arraignment, then I had a call they were on their way to the hospital to pick up Len who is being released"—she glanced at her wristwatch—"right about now."

"Poor Lenny. I hate that he was hurt."

"He'll be fine. Nasty whack on the head, but he wasn't completely knocked unconscious. Garrett and I followed the ambulance to the hospital and stayed until Lenny was comfortably settled." Milly returned to the task at hand, setting out lunch items.

"Thanks for making sure Emily was here for Evan when we got back. I'm concerned he's blaming himself for all of this. For not being more aware of Rhys's problems. Maybe even for Joan's death."

"Well, that's nonsense." Milly slammed a bowl of chicken salad on the counter. "Evan was better this morning. I think Emily helped him gain some perspective about this whole situation."

"Oh, that's good to hear. He really needed Emily last night."

"He did. She's a terrific young woman. Reminds me of you in a lot of ways." Milly placed plates, cutlery, and napkins on the counter.

"She's a good person, Mil. Evan needs her, and maybe they do have a future. Who knows?"

"As long as he doesn't confuse *need* with *love*. But I think he's smarter than that."

"I do, too." They heard the car drive up outside and car doors opening and closing.

Augusta watched as Milly deftly added glasses and beverages. "What would we do without you?"

"I have no idea," Milly replied, wiping her hands on a towel. "It's a damn good thing I came up here. You'd have all starved or died of thirst. Or both." Both women chuckled.

The group entered the house, talking quietly. Augusta went to her uncle, laying a gentle hand on his bandaged head. "Oh, Lenny. I'm so sorry this happened to you."

Len embraced his niece. "I'm fine. No concussion. It hurts but it will heal."

"I know Rhys hit you because you tried to stop him from going after me. My knight in shining armor."

Len grinned. "Hardly. I didn't stop him."

Mal stood behind Augusta, his hands on her shoulders. "You look rested, Mrs. Mitchell. Feeling better?"

"Much better, Detective Mitchell." Augusta turned to embrace him.

"I take it Rhys received a psych exam before the arraignment?" Milly asked.

"I requested an exam immediately after the preliminary hearing," Garrett explained. "I believe it will be enough for us to get him into a mental institution instead of being kept in jail, at least for the present. He didn't remember much about what happened last night, and even though he admits to seeing Joan the night she was killed, he swears he doesn't remember what happened. And he's pretty convincing."

"He's facing serious charges, though," Mal added. "This morning he was charged with Joan's murder as well as Augusta's kidnapping. When he was searched last night, a piece of jewelry was found on him. A bracelet."

"The bracelet Mrs. Cromer told Jim about," Augusta speculated. "The only way he could have it was if he took it from her that night. There is no way she would have given it to him."

"It's pretty damning evidence," Mal agreed.

"May I borrow a car?" Emily asked. "If you don't mind, I'd like to drive over to the cast house and collect the rest of my stuff."

"I can drive you," Evan offered.

"No, stay. I know you want to talk to Augusta."

"Don't you want to eat first?" Augusta asked, as her eyes met Emily's. *I like what's happening here*, she thought.

"I won't be long," Emily promised, pressing Evan's shoulder and dropping a soft kiss on his cheek before she left.

Plates were filled and drinks passed around. Augusta resumed her seat at the island and Evan sat next to her. She glanced around and noticed everyone else had made themselves scarce.

"I asked Mal and Garrett to give us a few minutes," Evan explained. "How are you really, Augusta? I can't begin to tell you how awful I feel about what happened…I feel responsible for the ordeal you endured last night."

"Well, *don't*. Don't do that to yourself, Evan. Rhys isn't your responsibility, not in any way. You have to realize how ill he is."

"That becomes more and more clear to me," Evan said. "Emily told me the same thing, that Rhys's behavior is a result of him being…wired wrong. She said nothing I might have said or done could have fixed that." He sighed. "She said it's obvious he's needed help for a long time and refused to recognize that he was in trouble."

"And you couldn't have known that. You've only seen him occasionally over the past twenty or so years."

"Yes, that's true. We haven't seen much of each other for a long time, not since I graduated from high school." He put his fork down. "I'm very lucky. I don't know that I could get through this without Emily."

Augusta studied his face. "You're going to be fine, Evan." She took a thoughtful sip of her iced tea. "Sometimes, out of the darkest moments, good things emerge. That happened to me with Mal when I first met him. I think I told you that he was lead detective for the murder of one of my voice students."

"And it was love at first sight?"

"Hardly." Augusta smiled wryly. "I was rude and obnoxious. I'll tell you the whole story sometime. But look where we are now."

Malcolm rejoined them. "Are you talking about me, Mrs. Mitchell?"

"About our past, Detective Mitchell. How I charmed you when we first met." They shared a smile, recalling the confrontation.

"What happened this morning at the arraignment, anyway?" Len said as he materialized on the other side of Evan.

"The arraignment took place in Mountainhome before the Barrett Township District Justice," Garrett replied, as he sat down next to Mal. "First, I met with the District Attorney of Monroe County, James Marse, for a preliminary hearing to discuss the charges. I requested a psychiatric examination of Rhys before he was brought in. Next, he was formally arraigned before the magistrate, and Mal was present for that."

"Where were Emily and Evan?" Milly asked, refilling drinks before she leaned against the counter.

"I decided it was better for them to not be there because of Rhys's state of mind, so they waited outside," Garrett replied. "Rhys is facing two charges. First, the murder of Joan Cromer. Second, the kidnapping and aggravated assault of Augusta. Either one is bad enough. It remains to be determined whether he'll be tried separately for each charge. However, given his mental condition, I don't foresee a trial for some time to come."

"How did you get him remanded to Lehigh River Hospital?" Len asked.

"That hasn't actually happened yet, but I'm sure it will be done soon," Garrett told them. "He should be moved within a day or two."

Milly poured him another cup of coffee. "Sounds to me like Rhys is getting the royal treatment. After he almost killed Augusta and Malcolm. And Evan. And I don't want to hear how mentally distraught he was."

"About charging him with Joan's murder," Mal said. "The evidence is all circumstantial, but it's still a strong case. Especially when the bracelet is factored in. And so far as the charges involving Augusta, there were plenty of witnesses who can attest to what happened last night."

Emily had returned and moved to stand beside Evan, a hand resting on his shoulder. "Whatever happens, Rhys will know you've done everything you can for him."

"Evan and Augusta need to get some rest if they are both still planning to perform tonight," Milly suggested.

Evan glanced at Augusta, who nodded. He stood. "Yes, we're performing, and a nap is essential."

An arm draped around Emily's shoulders, he glanced around the room. "Augusta said something to me earlier about light sometimes emerging from the darkest moments in our lives. I can't thank all of you enough for everything you've done." He smiled. "I think I've made some terrific new friends."

***

"I don't suppose there's any way you'd consider not performing tonight," Malcolm said, stretched out on the bed.

"You're right. I wouldn't." Augusta lay beside him, unable to relax. Images of the night before flashed through her mind no matter how she attempted to block them. Her frayed nerves caused her to twice adjust her position.

Mal leaned up on an elbow. "Do you need to talk?"

Augusta sat up, wrapping her arms around her knees. "What happened last night must have been something like being in a war zone. No wonder some soldiers come home with shell shock. I can't imagine going through that repeatedly."

She took a deep breath. "I've never been so…Mal, Rhys terrified me, from the moment he came into my dressing room. When he dragged me toward the mine entrance I nearly fainted. If you and Evan hadn't been there, I don't know what I would have done."

Augusta forced herself to keep her voice from rising as she stood and paced the room. "I'm so *angry* with him for what he put me—us—through. He may not be an inherently bad person; he's obviously mentally ill. But the fact remains he killed Joan. And he could have killed me. He could have killed all of us."

Mal took her hands and pulled her beside him on the bed, gently stroking her hair back. "We could speculate that he's partially a product of his environment. Miners are tough. Hard. They have to be. Rhys learned that not just from his family, but his entire community."

"You know, Rhys talked to me the entire time we were driving to Carbondale," Augusta said. "He had a difficult life, Mal. He hated the mines. You should have heard him; it was so apparent how miserable he had been." She gave a deep sigh. "Why didn't someone see the signs when he was younger? We know so little about diseases of the mind, and there is so much stigma attached to mental illness. I wonder how different Rhys might have been if he'd been allowed to follow the dream he saw Evan follow."

"There's no way to excuse what he did. He killed Joan Cromer. He could have killed you. There may be more he did that we don't know about."

"The way we look at mental illness is wrong. Or I should say the way we *don't* look at it. We ignore it. Sweep it under the rug. Pretend there's nothing happening. It's no wonder even if people realize they need help, they're reluctant to seek it. That has to change."

"Joan was disturbed as well. That was a contributing factor in her death." Malcolm leaned back and pulled Augusta close, stroking her shoulders. "You know, since you feel so strongly about this, you could make a difference. Get involved in advocating for better education about mental health. I know there must be a group in Cincinnati that would welcome the brilliant Professor McKee with open arms."

"I'll think about it. For now, though, I need to be onstage tonight." She felt tears blur her eyes. "I'm not...I almost lost myself. That's what he did to me." She angrily brushed the tears away.

Mal wrapped her in his strong arms and held her tightly. "I saw that last night, Gus. You had to know how worried I was."

"Yes, I did." She kissed his neck, finally relaxing into his arms. "I liked being pampered, I must say. You can do that any time. In fact, I insist on it. Once a week would be good."

"There's my fiery gypsy, Frasquita," Mal chuckled. "Get some rest, Gus. There may be thirty people on that stage tonight, but I'll only be watching this one."

Augusta lifted her face and kissed him, a long, lingering kiss, as she caressed the back of his neck.

"Enough talk, Detective Mitchell," she murmured.

"Copy that, Mrs. Mitchell."

Chapter 20
Lovers–Star-Crossed and Otherwise

Augusta walked into the Playhouse past a small knot of people who stopped talking abruptly and stared at her. She smiled at them, amused. *Oh, juicy gossip for sure.*

"Good to see you're performing tonight, Augusta," one ventured.

"Why wouldn't I be?" She breezed past them and heard murmurs and whispers. *They'll have their answers soon enough,* she thought.

She realized everyone in the Playhouse community, and at least some members of the audience, were aware of her absence from the stage in the final scene Wednesday night. No doubt some people were also aware that Rhys had abducted her. Augusta also surmised that at least a few residents of Mountainhome got wind of the arraignment before their magistrate, and that would have been a hot topic in Barrett Township.

The entire acting company—so consequently, the entire Playhouse staff, even volunteers—would know that Emily stayed overnight at Len Paynter's house. More speculation about exactly what that meant; they knew Evan had been staying there, and that Emily had been smitten with him since rehearsals began in New York.

No wonder they're gossiping, Augusta thought as she smiled to herself.

She found a replacement costume for her final appearance in the show and had just carried it into her dressing room when Emily tapped on the door and stuck her head in. "Evan is asking the company to meet briefly onstage at the 30-minute call. He wants to let them know what has happened."

"Sounds like an excellent idea. I'll be there."

Two minutes later, another tap, and Evan stepped inside. "Got a minute?"

"Of course. I hear you're planning to talk to the company."

"I have to. They need to know what's going on." He leaned against her dressing table. "Here's the thing, though. One question floating around is, why did Rhys abduct you? You and I—and Malcolm—know why. Rhys knew you were the one thing I wanted that I didn't get. But I don't think anyone else needs to know that."

"I agree. What did you have in mind?"

"Well, this is at least partly true. I want to tell them it's because you're Malcolm's wife, and Rhys knew the police were getting close to learning the truth. He panicked."

She thought for a moment. "I think it should work. I appreciate your discretion."

"Augusta…I need to say this, and it will be the last time I mention it. I was very much in love with you for a long time. Seeing you again awakened all those feelings. When you told me about Malcolm…that wasn't easy. But I want you to know this. Your husband is a great guy. And when I see the two of you together and what you have, I realize how right you are for each other."

Augusta had to take a moment to respond, feeling how close the tears were. "Evan, I hope you find the happiness you deserve. Truly."

***

Evan, with Emily at his side, glanced around the circle of cast and crew. He bent his head, then lifted it and took a deep breath. "Thanks for taking a few minutes to join me. I'm trying to come up with the right words here—to thank you for sticking with me while I was the number one suspect in a murder. It means a lot." Another breath. "Maybe some of you have heard that my cousin Rhys has been arrested and charged with Joan Cromer's murder."

A murmur around the circle, some nods, some shocked expressions. Evan continued, "This is really tough. It's…come to light that Rhys is a deeply disturbed man."

The circle was quiet. "You deserve to know what happened last night, why Augusta wasn't on stage at the end of the show. I think some of you know Rhys came backstage and kidnapped her." Murmurs and some muffled exclamations of shock from his listeners.

"Augusta's husband, Detective Mitchell, has been working on the case with the Pennsylvania State Police, and Rhys was aware of that. He panicked. Fortunately, the law enforcement officers were able to apprehend him before anyone was hurt."

He glanced at each of them. "I can't tell you how much I regret that any of this happened."

A soft female voice from the circle. "You don't have to say anything else. We get it." Another voice, this time one of the men. "We're with you, Evan."

Evan lowered his head again, and when he looked up his eyes were moist. "I just want to add that I've learned…we have to look out for the people we love. And sometimes, we need to urge them to get help. I wish I'd been able to do that for Rhys."

A few sniffs, and Augusta noticed some of the women wiping their eyes, as well as a couple of the men.

"You're not alone, Evan," Emily said as she took his hand. "You're never alone."

Assents and nods, and spontaneously the cast drew together for a prolonged group hug.

Their stage manager, Miles Richardson, stepped into the center of the circle. "Three more shows, folks. Let's give these audiences an experience they'll remember the rest of their lives. Let's make sure they never forget Billy Bigelow, the troubled soul, who is redeemed by the unwavering love of Julie Jordan."

The cast slowly and silently dispersed to get ready for the performance. Sounds drifted through the curtain as audience members began to enter the theater.

Augusta stood in the wings with Miles and they both looked toward center stage, where Evan and Emily were still wrapped in an embrace, his head on her shoulder.

"What about that?" Miles asked Augusta in a low voice. "Think they'll make it work?"

"At least for now. As for the future, who can say? I hope they find happiness together. But I'm often accused of being an incurable romantic."

***

In spite of the intense trauma of the previous night, or perhaps because of it, Augusta felt a heightened need to be on the stage—it was a way for her to find her way back from the edge.

The opening notes of "The Carousel Waltz" always caused her pulse to quicken and filled her with anticipation. Richard Rodgers had written it perfectly, she thought, the halting notes creating a sense of breathlessness, followed by the sweeping chords which started slowly as they represented the carousel beginning to turn.

She was caught up by the music, feeling a sense of joy—joy at being alive, being on this stage with these people, reliving this powerful story of love and redemption. As Nettie, she brought the children to the carousel and her eyes met Evan's. She saw he was experiencing the same emotions.

From the wings Augusta watched the scenes which followed, enthralled by the magic she was witnessing. Whenever Emily and Evan were on stage together, the performance that night was filled with a new ardor. Emily's love for Evan shone in every glance, every line of dialogue, every phrase of music.

Their solos in the Bench Scene—"If I Loved You"—shimmered with aching desire. When Evan sang to Emily, his eyes were alight with his growing love for her. *He looks so young*, Augusta thought. *Love will do that for you.*

At the end of the scene when the two of them watched the spring blossoms drifting to the stage, Billy reached up and caught one, placing it behind Julie's ear, and Evan and Emily kissed, a full lover's kiss, holding nothing back, as the lights dimmed and the curtain came down.

The entire cast became caught up in what was for many of them the most extraordinary experience they'd ever had in a performance. They weren't acting, they were living this story. As well as he had performed the "Soliloquy" in previous performances, Evan outdid himself and the applause from the audience was prolonged.

The story continued, and the audience fell in love with Julie as they never had before. When Emily sang "What's the Use of Wonderin'," Julie's declaration of her love for Billy, no matter what might happen, Augusta could observe Evan watching Emily from the wings as if he were seeing her for the first time. The song epitomized what the story was really about—Julie's steadfast, unfaltering love for Billy. *Evan has to realize Emily is singing this to him,* Augusta thought. She had a sense of watching their love story unfolding before her eyes, and it gave her a feeling of peace. *He's going to be all right.*

Julie's farewell speech to Billy after he died in her arms was so poignant there were some tears from the actors on stage as well as in the audience. Nettie comforted Julie after Billy's death, singing the song that had become a classic in musical theater, "You'll Never Walk Alone."

Augusta had sung the song many times, even before this run of the show, but tonight she experienced it on a different level. She felt herself a conduit for all the emotion, hope, and love it so beautifully expressed.

She stayed in the wings with Emily to hear Evan sing "The Highest Judge of All." The two women moved to their dressing rooms during the ballet to change their costumes for the final scenes.

Augusta had managed to put Rhys Llewellyn out of her mind, but she had a bad moment as she walked into her dressing room. A chill ran through her as she vividly recalled Rhys abruptly stepping inside the room, gun pointed directly at her. She managed to shake it off, but it was a reminder that what she had experienced wouldn't soon fade.

At the very end of the show when Billy, who was invisible to Julie, spoke to her, Evan changed the line slightly. First, he declared his love for her, and the scripted line continued, "Know that I loved you." Instead, he concluded, "I will always love you." And Emily added a gesture, touching his unseen face lightly as her eyes shone. He left the stage with the Heavenly Starkeeper as the cast sang the final lines of "You'll

Never Walk Alone," their voices filling the theater with passionate elation.

The standing-room-only audience gave the show a ten-minute ovation, and calls of "Julie! Billy! Julie!" rang through the theater. Evan pulled his lady forward and started the renewed applause for her. Overcome, Emily sank down on one knee, head bowed, tears on her face.

The curtain descended one final time. Cast members wept and hugged each other, overcome with emotion. When Mal came backstage Augusta ran to him, clinging to him without words.

He held her tightly. "Now it's over, Gus. You've come through to the other side." He tipped her chin up and gazed into her face. "My magnificent Augusta."

***

Len Paynter and his house guests made a point of slipping away quickly after the performance. They were exhilarated by what they had just experienced, but they were also exhausted—physically, mentally, and emotionally. When they arrived back at Len's, they seemed reluctant to go inside, lingering on the porch for a time, enjoying the quiet, the starlit night, and the fresh, cool air.

Milly went to the kitchen with Len, and the two of them quickly set out snacks and beverages. "I know you all need sleep, but you probably need a little sustenance before you turn in," Milly said. "I have to say, I've never seen anything like the show you just did. I didn't want it to end."

"Agreed," Len said. "Absolutely magical. And after what you went through last night. How in the world did you do that?"

Evan wrapped an arm around Emily's waist, pulled her close and gazed at her. "It was pretty magical."

"Who can explain it?" Augusta answered. "It was like a gift. A gift we gave each other and the audience."

"You performers, get upstairs and get some sleep. You've earned it," Garrett said, as he gathered up glasses and plates.

"Is it okay if I take my detective? I sleep better when he's close by," Augusta said, making them all laugh.

***

Friday was a day of rest for Len's guests, and they took full advantage of it. Garrett was able to visit Rhys at the Lehigh River Hospital in the afternoon. Rhys seemed to vaguely understand where he was and why he was there. Garrett and Milly had plane tickets back to Cincinnati Saturday morning. Mal and Augusta's travel day would be Sunday, after the final performance of *Carousel* Saturday night at Pocono Playhouse.

Friday night, their next-to-last performance, Evan's Carbondale contingent attended the show. Evan had heard from his parents that shock waves ran through his family's circle of friends when they learned of Rhys's illness and arrest. Evan wasn't sure what to expect, but Augusta was thrilled to see the strong support they offered him. She felt the emotions she saw on their faces—love, pride, concern. It was apparent Evan was deeply moved.

At an after-party previously planned at a nearby family resort, Augusta and Malcolm circulated for a while and listened to the chatter. Shock and sadness for Rhys. Praise for Evan. Speculation about Emily, since it was obvious that she and Evan were together.

Once back at Lenny's, Mal stretched out on the bed and Augusta lay beside him.

"I've been doing a lot of thinking," she said, leaning up on one elbow. "What happened to us Wednesday night was the most frightening event of my life. And when you said you were afraid you might lose me…well, it's made me think of all you've done trying to protect me. I know if anything really bad had happened to me— if I'd been seriously injured, or killed—it would have meant that for the rest of your life, you would carry an awful burden because you weren't able to protect me." She saw a muscle work in Mal's jaw.

"I never want to put you through that again." Augusta lay down and pulled her husband into her arms. "I know I can't promise, but I can certainly make every effort to stay away from potentially dangerous situations."

Mal was quiet for a moment. "Don't blame yourself for the things that have happened to you," he said. "Especially Wednesday night. Or really, not for any of the experiences we've shared over the last three years."

"Well, there have been times I meddled when I shouldn't have. Or didn't tell you things when I should

276

have. I can try my best to avoid repeating that kind of behavior."

He gazed into her eyes and smiled. "Gus, I wouldn't want you any other way than who you are."

Content, she sighed and pressed herself close to him.

***

Mal met George LaBar for breakfast Saturday morning, and the men promised to keep in touch. Augusta and Malcolm had canceled their proposed hike of Mt. Tammany later that day; her leg was healing but still sore. Instead, Lenny offered to take Augusta and Mal and Evan and Emily out onto the Delaware River. A friend who lived near the village of Shawnee-on-Delaware had canoes they could borrow, and when they arrived at Smithfield Beach, he had tied two together for them. The plan was to drift down the river through the Water Gap to a point just north of Portland, on the Pennsylvania side of the river. It seemed an ideal way to end what had been an incredibly stressful nine days.

"You know Emily and I went to the Lehigh River Hospital this morning to see Rhys," Evan said. "It seems like a good place. Staffed by caring and skilled people."

"Rhys has remembered some of what happened Wednesday night," Emily added. "He asked us to tell both of you how sorry he was. He said someday he hopes to apologize to Augusta in person."

"I know he's very ill." Augusta trailed one hand in the clear, cool water of the Delaware. "I hope he receives the help he needs." *Sorry, Evan. That's the best I can do right now.*

The boats rocked slightly as they continued drifting southward, lulling them into a blissful, relaxed state of laziness.

After a moment Evan asked, "What about that story you promised to tell me. About the first time you two met?"

"Oh, that," Augusta laughed. "Let's see…Detective Mitchell wouldn't allow me on the campus at Cliffside College where my student had been murdered. Only of course, I didn't know that was the reason he was playing dragon at the gate."

"Professor McKee tried very hard to intimidate me," Mal said, with a grin. "Needless to say, she failed."

"But I fixed him. I knew a back way onto the campus. I had to take off my stilettos and throw them over a four-foot rock wall so I could climb it, but a few minutes later there I was, walking toward him in those stilettos."

They all laughed. "And then?" asked Emily.

"How could I resist such a resourceful, beautiful, fascinating woman?" Mal replied. "By the end of the morning she was helping me interview students."

"And the first time I saw him smile—really smile— I was hooked. That smile and those amazing blue eyes."

"And the rest is history," Mal added.

Lenny gestured up ahead. "This is what we're here to see, I believe."

They watched in silence as the Gap came into sight. In awe, they stared up at Mt. Tammany and Mt. Minsi, conscious that the river they were floating on had at one time—many millennia past—flowed where the tops of those cliffs loomed now. Drifting into and through the Gap gave an entirely new perspective of its magnificent beauty.

***

"What will happen with them, do you think—Emily and Evan?" Mal asked as they lay wrapped in each other's arms after the final *Carousel* performance that night. The cast had performed to another standing-room-only audience that didn't want to let them go.

"You know, I think they'll be married within six months. And I think they'll have ups and downs, just as everyone does, but I believe it will be a strong marriage. I'm happy for them."

"My bride, ever the romantic," Mal chuckled. "I hope you're right." He leaned back and grinned. "The age difference doesn't seem like an issue to you?"

"What age difference? Chronological or emotional? Emily is ages older than Evan emotionally."

Mal sat up abruptly. "Who are you and what have you done with my wife?" he demanded, his blue eyes twinkling.

Augusta pulled him down. "Oh, shush. Do you want me to tell you that you were right? I can do that. You were right. You're ages older than I am."

He laughed again and kissed her warmly. "It will be great to get home."

"It definitely will. Wonder if Fritz will even remember us?" She nestled closely against him. "Len will miss us, though. He loved having us here."

"Well, he's coming to Cincinnati for Thanksgiving and staying through Christmas. And we'll be back here next summer. We still have to climb Mt. Tammany. And another trip up Mt. Minsi. We'll bring Fritz with us next time we come."

"Now, that will be an adventure," Augusta laughed.

Mal leaned on one elbow, an eyebrow lifted. "Adventure? A 'potentially dangerous situation'? I thought you were planning to avoid those in the future."

"Well, I didn't exactly say that. Who knows what the future holds, Detective Mitchell? And maybe the Italians have it right."

"How's that?"

"*Qualunque cosa debba accadere accadrà.*"

"Which means…?"

"Whatever is meant to happen, will happen." She kissed his shoulder.

Mal chuckled. "Wasn't there a song about that in some movie?"

"I think it had a different title. I like mine better. Anyway, let's go to Italy soon."

Mal laughed heartily and pulled the covers over both their heads.

ACKNOWLEDGMENTS

In the previous book in "The Augusta McKee Mystery Series," *The Case of the Unearthed Evidence,* Augusta and Malcolm spent a short getaway weekend in the Pocono Mountains of Pennsylvania. The logical next step was for them to solve a mystery during a second visit. And the wonderful old summer theater, The Pocono Playhouse, was a perfect setting. I spent many happy hours watching outstanding productions there which featured New York casts during the 1970s and early 1980s.

The Playhouse was sold in the mid-1980s and through a series of misfortunes lost its professional (Equity) standing. However, many enjoyable summer productions, largely with local talent, continued until the building was set on fire and burned to the ground in 2009. But that's another story, and it was my great pleasure to resurrect the Playhouse as it was in its "glory" days, and to give Augusta an opportunity to perform in one of my favorite musical dramas, *Carousel.*

I'm much indebted once again to retired Lt. Det. Stephen Kramer, Cincinnati Police Department, for his input in those scenes involving the CPD, and as always, his approval of actions and thoughts of fictional Homicide Detective Malcolm Mitchell. I also must thank yet another member of law enforcement, retired Pennsylvania State trooper, Tpr. First Class George Kerrick, for his generous assistance in explaining what I needed to learn about how the Pennsylvania State Police operate and how my fictional State Trooper George LaBar would respond and react to the events in this story. And I thank the real George for allowing me to give my fictional trooper his first name. It was fun to get positive reactions from both the real law enforcement officers to my scenes between my fictional characters!

As always, a vital part of the conception and development of this book was my more-than-editor, Ashleigh Evans. We developed the plot of this book through an exchange of ideas. However, as I began writing the early chapters, Ashleigh went through a difficult medical crisis. I am forever grateful that she eventually made a full recovery, and was here to guide the book to its conclusion.

We work quite closely together and it wasn't easy not to have her input. I must especially thank two dear friends and writers who have been my mentors since I first started on this journey some eight years ago. Michaele Benedict and Eric Mark kindly stepped in and gave me encouragement and guidance during Ashleigh's unexpected absence. They were as thrilled as I was when she was able to return to put her firm hand on the tiller.

Ashleigh once again kept a tight rein on my tendencies to sometimes move too far toward romance. When Augusta remarks she's "often considered an incurable romantic" in the final chapter, she's echoing thoughts my intrepid editor has expressed about me on more than one occasion.

Eric is an avid climber of Mt. Minsi, and he assisted me in developing the scene of Augusta and Mal's climb.

Thanks also to my son Steve, another lover of the Water Gap, for his thoughts on the climb, and on the cliffs.

Members of the Pocono theater community will recognize the name of the wardrobe mistress in this story, "Laurie Benefield," as a composite of two exceptional costumers I was privileged to work with frequently when I directed some eighty productions of community and high school musicals—my tribute to Laurie Favini and Missy Benefield, who are also dear friends.

I'm not sure why I decided Evan Llewellyn should come from a coal mining community not far from the Poconos. (On the other hand, I think along with many writers I have a sense my characters present themselves to me in often mysterious ways.) Researching the history of Carbondale and underground coal mining was fascinating and engrossing, and I was fortunate to have a friend and neighbor, Richard Waibel, who was a native of Carbondale and could give me that special insight into being a part of the community during the time the underground fire was being excavated.

Thanks as always to my generous readers for their suggestions and corrections: Ken Van Camp, Amy Cramer, Matthew Hendry, Audrey Henry, Marti Lantz, and Nathaniel Taylor. They are a vital part of my process and I know the book is better and stronger because of their interest.

Taylor Van Kooten has once again provided a creative and imaginative cover for this seventh book in the series, and as always, I admire and appreciate her artistry.

And finally, my thanks to my wonderful friends, the Lady Writers of the Poconos, who offered thoughts about several scenes and gave me support and encouragement throughout the process: Sahar Abdulaziz, Belinda Gordon, Evelyn Infante, Kelly Jensen, Mary Anne Moore, and Catherine Schratt.

Though *The Case of the 'Carousel' Killer* is set in the mid-1960s, it was written in the midst of the COVID-19 pandemic, and the effects of that epidemic on everyone, the author included, were difficult to block out. This Augusta portrayal feels more vulnerable than in earlier books, more aware of the vagaries of life.

It will be interesting to see where life takes Augusta and Malcolm next.

Susan Moore Jordan
Spring, 2021
Pocono Mountains

VIDEOGRAPHY

These videos were available on YouTube
as of May 2021

"The Carousel Waltz" – Proms 2010
    John Wilson Orchestra
    John Wilson, conductor

"The Bench Scene (If I Loved You)" – Live from
Lincoln Center, 2013
    Nathan Gunn, baritone, as Billy Bigelow
    Kelli O'Hara, soprano, as Julie Jordan

"Soliloquy"—Live from Lincoln Center, 2013
    Nathan Gunn as Billy

"What's the Use of Wonderin'" –Live from Lincoln
Center, 2013
    Kelli O'Hara as Julie

"You'll Never Walk Alone" –2018 Broadway Cast
Recording
    Renée Fleming, soprano, as Nettie

"This Nearly Was Mine" from *South Pacific*
Carnegie Hall
    Brian Stokes Mitchell, baritone, as Emile

"Sixteen Tons" by Merle Travis
    Performed by Tennessee Ernie Ford

The Case of the
Slain Soprano

Chapter 1
A Death on Campus

Augusta turned her brand-new 1963 sapphire blue Chrysler Imperial onto Victory Parkway almost automatically. She made this drive four days a week, sometimes after lunch, sometimes at eight in the morning as she did this particular Thursday.

Traffic on the always busy Parkway, a major artery on the eastern side of Cincinnati, was unusually slow this April morning, and it became a crawl as she neared the entrance to Cliffside College. The reason for the tie-up immediately became apparent: four police cars—one a station wagon—and an ambulance were lined up along the entrance. Oncoming traffic was being directed into another lane to move past the school's entrance. Augusta had on her left turn indicator and was approached by a police officer.

He waited for her to roll down her window. "Sorry, ma'am. No one is permitted on the campus at this time."

"Nonsense. I'm a faculty member. I have classes and private voice lessons to teach this morning." Augusta stared him down.

"I have my orders, ma'am. I'm afraid I can't allow you to turn."

Augusta turned off the engine. "I wish to speak with the person who gave you those orders, officer. I'm not moving."

The police officer returned quickly, accompanied by a dark-haired man some might consider ruggedly attractive, dressed in slightly rumpled plain clothes. *Startlingly blue eyes. Over six feet, I would guess. Fortyish.*

"Good morning, ma'am. I'm going to have to ask you to move on."

"I can't do that, Detective," Augusta said, guessing his rank. "I'm due in class at nine."

"Detective Mitchell, ma'am. No classes today."

"Why? What's happened?"

"There's been a death in Emery Hall."

Augusta felt herself blanch. *Dear God.* "A student?"

"I really can't give you that information. And I must insist you move on, or you may find yourself under arrest."

Augusta opened the car door and stepped out to face the detective. She was nearly as tall as he was and knew how intimidating she could be when she chose. "And I must insist you tell me what has happened here." She fished in her purse for identification. "The police chief is a personal friend. Call him and tell him Professor Augusta McKee requests admission to the Cliffside College campus. Immediately."

"Ma'am, I'm not calling anyone. *You* can call whomever you choose, including the Pope. I cannot allow you on campus." He folded his arms across his chest and raised an eyebrow.

Asshole, she thought, a word she would never have spoken aloud. *We'll see about that.*

"Very well, detective…may I have your name?" Augusta opened her car door as she spoke.

"Malcolm Mitchell. May I have yours?"

"Professor Augusta McKee. I just told you. Apparently, you weren't paying attention." She slammed the door. "Be assured—the police chief will hear about this." Icicles dripped from every word.

"Oh, I have no doubt about it." He gave her an insolent grin as she drove away.

Undeterred, Augusta turned around and headed back up Victory Parkway. She made her way through quiet residential back streets to a little dead-end cul-de-sac where she parked, exited her car, and started down a path.

She stepped carefully in her Roger Vivier stilettos along the partially cleared wooded path. About a half mile beyond the dead-end street, she came to a four-foot stone wall with clearly visible foot and hand holds.

Augusta was hardly dressed for scaling a wall, but the coral dress she had on—a favorite—had a skirt full enough for her to pull the front and back together between her legs and tie it loosely but securely. She slipped off her shoes and tossed them over the wall. Stepping carefully so as not to snag her stockings, she easily climbed up and over the wall, untied her skirt, reclaimed her shoes, and walked the remaining half mile to the back of the campus, behind the greenhouse. Pulling herself up to her full five feet nine inches (plus the additional three the stilettos provided) she sailed past the police stationed near the greenhouse, breathing a small sigh of relief when none of them challenged her presence.

Some of the Sisters of Mercy who were on the staff of the school were standing around in little knots of three or four, not speaking. One of the younger nuns, Sister Mary David, hurried to speak to Augusta.

"Oh, Professor McKee, it's so, so, so sad. Linnea Murphy fell down the stairs and hit her head ... and died." *Linnea?* Augusta was quite taken aback. Before she had a chance to respond Detective Mitchell strode toward her, obviously dumbfounded.

"I guess there's no point in my asking how you got here," he remarked, shaking his head.

Augusta flashed the detective her most charming smile. "Now that I'm here, I appeal to you not to throw me off campus. I assure you I can be of help to you, but I would like to know exactly what happened here that requires your presence."

Against his better judgment, he relented. "I suppose the good Sister gave you some information." Augusta nodded. "Linnea Murphy was found dead this morning at the bottom of a flight of stairs in the residence hall."

Augusta flinched. "I see."

"There seem to have been no witnesses."

"Accident?"

He paused briefly before he replied, "The cause of her death remains unknown at the present time."

"You're a homicide detective, then. Foul play hasn't been ruled out."

She caught the slight smirk and was certain he viewed her as some kind of amateur sleuth in the Miss Marple mold.

"Don't worry, Detective. I won't interfere with your duties."

***

"Thank you, Professor McKee," said Detective Edmonds. "We appreciate your assistance." He said to his partner, "I'll let the officers outside know we're wrapping things up here."

Detective Mitchell nodded and turned to Augusta. "This is tough for these girls."

"Yes, it is. I'm concerned about Eileen in particular."

"She mentioned the college's upcoming musical production. You direct it, right?"

"How did you know that?"

"I'm a detective, Professor. I just did a little detecting." He gave her a crooked grin and ran a hand through the back of his dark hair.

"You called Chief Schrotel, didn't you?" She felt a smile tugging at her lips. *Well, what do you know? The detective can be rather charming.*

"Guilty as charged." He raised his hands in mock surrender. "He spoke highly of you and suggested you would probably be very helpful."

Augusta managed not to say *I told you so.* "Stan Schrotel is one of the most remarkable people I've ever known, but I'm sure as a member of his force you are well aware of that."

"We all know we have a great role model, Professor. I feel privileged to serve under his command."

He smiled warmly as he spoke. *My word, when he smiles like that he's downright handsome.*

"Good luck with your show, Professor. What are you doing, by the way?"

"Gilbert and Sullivan. *The Pirates of Penzance*." Augusta's mind was immediately engaged by the problems looming ahead of her.

"I have to go this way." She gestured toward the greenhouse, then shook both detectives' hands. "Good luck, gentlemen."

As Augusta walked away she managed a glance back, pleased to see Malcolm Mitchell watching her leave as he leaned against his car.

After a lifetime as a musician—performer, teacher, musical theater director—Susan Moore Jordan wrote and published her first novel in 2013 at the age of seventy-five, and she hasn't stopped since.

In her first four novels, the author drew from her life experiences as a voice teacher and stage director, and those historical novels were inspired by real people she encountered.

"Companion" novels, *Memories of Jake* and *Man with No Yesterdays* were released in March and November of 2017. A departure from her earlier historical novels, these two books detail the struggles of two brothers, Andrew and Jake Cameron, whose lives were irrevocably changed by their service in the Vietnam War. *Memories of Jake* was the recipient of an honorable mention Red Ribbon Award from the 2017 Wishing Shelf Book Awards. *Man with No Yesterdays* was a Finalist in the 2019 Wishing Shelf Book Awards, and Semi-Finalist in the 2020 Kindle Book Awards.

More recently, Jordan has embarked on a "cozy mystery" series, "The Augusta McKee Mysteries." A complete list of the books in the series can be found in the front of this book. *The Case of the Slain Soprano* was a finalist in the 2018 Wishing Shelf Book Awards and a semi-finalist for the 2020 Kindle Book Awards. *The Case of the Disappearing Director* was a finalist in the 2019 Wishing Shelf Book Awards.

All of Jordan's books are "music-centric" (in the words of one reviewer), and readers comment on the strength of the element of music included in her work. Jordan sees writing as another way to share the music she loves, which she considers "the most powerful force in the universe."

Articles by Susan Moore Jordan have appeared in *Musical America* and *The Guardian*, and on August 2, 2019, she appeared on Hour Three of "The Today Show" as a Super Senior.

***

If you enjoyed
The Case of the 'Carousel' Killer,
please consider leaving a reader review on Amazon. Reviews are a standing ovation! They are also valuable to indie authors
and are greatly appreciated.
More information and links to all my books
can be found on my website,
www.susanmoorejordan.com